52 STORIES IN 2023

VOLUME ONE

MICHAEL KINGSWOOD

CONTENTS

Introduction   v

Midwatch Asylum   1

Spirit Foreclosure   23

Odin's Peppermint   55

A Nose For Tacos   85

Cosmic Pizza   99

Crowned Emperor   125

Miss Melody And The Jail Cell   145

Watching Big Ben   163

Eyes Of Gold   179

Dream Of The Dryad   199

Kickstarter Heroes   221
Message From The Author   223
Mailing List   225
About The Author   227
More Books By Michael Kingswood   229

INTRODUCTION

Every year I set goals for my writing in order to push myself to improve both my craft and my production. For 2023 I committed to writing at least one piece of short fiction every week, and to put them out in five collections over the course of the year. To make it more interesting, I also committed to running crowdfunding campaigns for each of the collections.

This is the first collection to come out of this challenge. It consists of ten stories ranging from military science fiction to sweet, meet-cute romance, and I had a lot of fun writing them. They are presented in the order they were written.

Have fun reading these stories, and I hope you'll join me for the remaining four collections of 2023.

Warm Regards,
Michael Kingswood

May 2023
San Diego, CA

MIDWATCH ASYLUM

As a retired Naval Officer, I enjoy reading military science fiction books. But I also sometimes find them frustrating, because I compare how the authors portray a Navy against what I experienced, and they often come up lacking.

Which of course means I have to write military science fiction of my own.

This first story follows the adventures of a flight crew in the Icaran Confederation Navy, which I created to scratch that military scifi itch. I've written a number of stories featuring the ICN, and intend to write many more going forward.

Enjoy!

W hen you look out into the depths of the endless night of space, it's easy to lose yourself. The soul-imperiling emptiness stretching for inconceivable distances in all directions. The stark beauty of the multitudinous, yet also somehow exceedingly rare by volume, stars everywhere.

Every time Lieutenant Jason Hensen, Icaran Confederation Navy, looked out there, he had to force himself to not wander into an awed stupor, just gazing into nothing and everything and leaving the world behind in rapturous contemplation of the stupefying immensity of it, and his minuscule to the point of meaninglessness position within it.

Fortunately, the piloting bubble of the surveillance and reconnaissance skiff he flew had a heads-up display built into the plasteel hemisphere surrounding his pilot's station. The skiff's course vector ran ahead, a deep blue line with pips denoting her current velocity, and a smaller red or green line showing the current acceleration he had applied. The icons showing the locations of nearby vessels—blue circles for navy, green squares for civilian, yellow squares for unknown—were also projected in locations on the bubble corresponding to their current positions, smaller numerical values depicting whether those locations were from the skiff's sensors, the star system's Common Operating Picture (COP), or from the vessels' transponders. The star system's ecliptic was a white line drawn across the whole, with planets and other large objects shown as solid white circles.

More than enough to keep him from zoning out too badly.

Most of the time.

But when he had the midwatch patrol, even that wasn't always enough. Not much ever happened on the midwatch.

Most of the time.

And this night wasn't shaping up to be much different. Except...

The slightly bitter scent on the air from the atmosphere processing gear back aft seemed more sharp than normal just then, and Jason's malaise eased as he perked up in his seat, the olive-green flight suit he wore rustling softly from his sudden movement. His eyes flicked up and to the right, to where his ship's status display was projected on the piloting bubble.

Internal pressure and temperature—always just a tiny bit on the chilly side for his taste—both read normal. Fuel status was as expected for this long into the patrol. Reactor output was also to be expected for his throttle setting.

"Boxer, you seeing anything abnormal in ship's systems?" he asked.

He didn't wear a headset. His implants detected the speech automatically and transmitted it through the skiff's internal communications system to his Sensor And Auxiliary Systems Operator (SASO) in the body of the skiff astern of him.

In the older models that Jason had initially trained on before hitting the Fleet Replacement Squadron and then SSR-25, the Timberwolves, the SASO would have sat directly to his right, making comms easier. But they lacked the all-around piloting bubble, instead being configured more like the cockpit of an atmospheric transport.

Jason preferred it this way. And anyway Boxer was close enough that they could hear each other just fine unless they had the hatch from the hull to the piloting bubble shut, and they only did that during combat conditions. The implants were just backups most of the time.

"Negative, Joyride. Everything's in the green. Why?"

No matter how many times he heard it, Jason's callsign made him chuckle ruefully and shake his head. He should never have told the guys about that incident. Ah well.

He rolled his shoulders and blew out a breath to clear the imagined cobwebs and re-focus himself. "Nothing, I guess. Just imagining things."

"Yeah well, it's the midwatch. Want some tunes?"

Jason glanced to the left and up, to his Navigation overlay box. He had set the home waypoint to ICS HATHERLY, the ship he and his flight detachment were based aboard, and they were currently 80,000 clicks away and getting farther by the moment.

Playing music over the internal comms system was contrary to regulations, but what the hell. It was the midwatch, and HATHERLY was far enough away who would know?

"A little metal never hurts."

Boxer groaned slightly; he was more into operatic and classical music. But Jason was the spacecraft commander, and anyway Boxer had picked the tunes last time. So a moment later a pounding bass line accompanied by hard drums and a hard, syncopated guitar riff began piping through his implants.

Softly, so as to not drown out official comms. But it made all the difference.

The night's mission profile was a standard forward scouting pattern: go out 300k clicks ahead of HATHERLY's planned track on passive sensors then reposition to four points 100k to port and starboard, above and below the track, and initiate active scans at each point.

Passive gravitic sensors combined with inputs from the COP and transponder feeds from civilian vessels should provide a clear picture of activity half a million clicks or more ahead of HATHERLY's track for the duration of the patrol, farther than HATHERLY could see with her onboard passive sensors. The brief active scans would pick up anything the passive scans missed. The skiff would send updated track reports through their data link with the ship, so the Tactical

Action Officer (TAO) there could better decide how to go about the night's mission.

HATHERLY could, of course, run active scans of her own, but that had the potential of giving her position away. And their tasking was to remain undetected as far as feasible while maintaining safety of ship. So she was running with her transponder in receive-only mode and using the skiffs from the flight detachment as her eyes and ears.

That meant some risk to Jason and Boxer, because when they did their scans their emissions would be detectable to other vessels. But the skiff's active array was turned to frequencies used by commonly carried civilian sensors so that risk was minimal.

Or so the geeks who designed them said. But they weren't out here on the edge of the Tsago Dominance's space, with their butts on the line.

Not that there was a shooting war at the moment. Or indication that there might be. But relations with the Dominance had never been good after the disastrous first encounter between their ships and those of the Icaran Confederation. In the two decades since then, there had been a number of small border skirmishes that only heavy lifting from the Diplomatic Corps had stopped from turning into something more.

And the Dominance had swallowed up two independent systems that the government on Icarus knew of during that time period. So there was always that possibility in the back of everyone's mind.

But it was the midwatch. And Dominance personnel were human too; they had to sleep like everyone else.

Didn't mean they had to keep their ships clocks set to the system's local standard, though. Their midwatch might be HATHERLY's noon.

Comforting thought.

Ahead and to port, twenty degrees depressed from the skiff's course vector and 450,000 clicks distant, was the jump point into Dominance space. Tonight's patrol would bring Jason and Boxer within weapons range of any vessel that might be lurking nearby there or that jumped into the system.

Long weapons range, and evasion wouldn't be all that difficult from such a long shot. But the danger was not zero.

So it was with some trepidation that he watched the range ticker to their first patrol waypoint tick down toward zero over the next half hour. He throttled back, lowering the skiff's speed to match HATHERLY's as they arrived, then did a quick scan of the contact icons on his piloting bubble. All green, no yellow. And no red.

"We've reached Point One," he said. "Anything?"

Boxer replied quickly, "Nope. Commending active scan."

"Roger," Jason said, and felt himself tense up slightly.

Of course, there was no reason to get nervous. No Dominance ships were in system, or scheduled to come visit. Or at least, the Diplomats didn't know of any that they had passed on to the Navy.

Didn't mean there couldn't be a surprise waiting.

But five minutes later, Boxer reported no new contacts, so Jason adjusted course for the second patrol waypoint.

And then after detecting nothing again at the second waypoint, Jason put those little bits of nervousness aside with a wry, silent self-scold. Of course nothing was going to happen. It was the midwatch.

And it was over halfway done. He glanced up at the chronometer tucked away in his ship's status display box, and despite having gotten a good crew rest before takeoff, had to fight to suppress a yawn. 0332. Their relief would be launching in an hour and a half, and then they could head back to the barn a half hour later, once Jerky and Hobo got on station.

It was going to be a long couple of hours. If—

A burst of light below and to the right of him drew Jason's eye. Adrenaline surged through him as he got a full look at it: a kaleidoscope of colors throughout the visible spectrum, wavering and turning in space for a couple seconds, and then just as quickly winking out as though it had never been.

"Gravitic sensors just pegged," Boxer reported, surprise plain in his voice.

"The jump point opened."

"Say again?"

"Commence active scan."

"Joyride—"

"Do it!"

A few seconds passed, then Boxer replied in the kind of a clipped, professional tone that he only used when he was really feeling the stress. "New contact bearing 035 mark 062," and a white block appeared on the piloting bubble right where the swath of light from the jump point opening had been. "No transponder. Course..." Boxer paused. "Course is erratic, fluctuating."

"Can you get a visual?" Unless the craft, whatever it was, was significantly smaller than the skiff, they should be well within resolution range on one of the two optical telescopes mounted on the skiff's dorsal and ventral surfaces.

"Wait one."

In his mind's eye Jason could see Boxer working the controls to bring the lower camera online and align it to the contact. Should be just a—

Boxer let out a low whistle. "Check it out."

A data window popped up on the piloting bubble. Jason felt his eyebrows rising of their own accord and his jaw drop open. "What is that?"

Data on the Dominance's Naval Order of Battle was far

from complete, but he had learned the silhouettes of all their known craft. This didn't match any of them.

It was tough to tell scale for certain, but Jason would bet the craft was not very much larger than his skiff. It was triangular, with what on an atmospheric craft would be called a delta wing. And it had a vertical stabilizer as well. Maybe it was designed for both orbital and atmospheric flight?

It was painted sky blue except for on the leading surfaces of the delta wing, which were charcoal grey, and it had an intricate design in red, green, and black on the side of its vertical stabilizer. Green and red running lights shown from the starboard and port wingtips, as per standard, and it had a red strobe atop the stabilizer and a pair of solid white lights on the dorsal section of its hull.

And it was spinning: a slow counterclockwise yaw that made it almost resemble a misshapen top from this angle. And no wonder. A significant portion of the trailing edge of the port delta wing had been blown off, looked like. There were black scorch marks all over, anyway. A whitish mist trailed behind the craft as it spun: off-gassing of some sort.

"Dunno. But it looks like he took a hit," Boxer said, echoing Jason's thoughts.

"Yeah. Did you pass the word to HATHERLY?"

"Affirm. They're setting Condition 2 and adjusting course to intercept, flank acceleration. Jerky and Hobo are up and starting launch preps."

For all the good that would do. The flight detachment had been maintaining Alert 60 per standard peacetime procedures: ready to launch in an hour from call-up. Jerky and Hobo might be able to go faster than that since they would have already started their preflight preparations for their scheduled patrol. But probably not by much.

The closest other naval units were halfway around the

system to spinward, and even though HATHERLY was now burning toward them at 15 Gs, she wouldn't get here for longer than it would take Jerky and Hobo to launch.

So Jason and Boxer were on their own for a while.

"Ok. I'm going to maneuver us closer. Try hailing it."

"It's moving away from the jump point pretty quickly; must have been burning like hell on the other side. But we won't just be within weapons range from the jump point when we reach it; we'll almost be at point blank range."

"It's a vessel in distress. We can't just leave it."

A short pause, then Jason could practically hear Boxer's nod, see his rueful grimace. "Yeah. Just saying."

"I know. Get the countermeasures system warmed up, and tell HATHERLY we're moving in."

"I turned it on as soon as the jump point opened."

Jason smiled grimly at that, then he adjusted the control yoke to point the skiff toward the tactical system's computed intercept point with the new contact—shown as a grey circle offset from the contact box by about 30 degrees—and increased the thrust from the skiff's gravitic engines.

As he did so, Boxer sent out, "Unknown craft exiting the Jinhua Jump Point, this is the Icaran Confederation Navy Skiff Lobo Six Zero Seven, approaching from forward starboard at 30 degrees elevation. You are directed to identify yourself, over," on the common hailing frequency.

It was the standard frequency used in all of the Confederation's systems, and all the other nations the Confederation dealt with. Even the Dominance used it, though not in their home systems. So there was a decent chance the intruder could receive the transmission, or at least know to tune to that frequency.

But then if this wasn't a Dominance ship, maybe not? And would they understand the language? The Dominance primarily used Mandarin, and a bit of Cantonese and Nihongo, but they could speak the common English that the Confederation and her neighbors used, and did when they interacted with the ICN. But who knew what this guy spoke.

"One thing at a time," Jason said to himself, earning a "Huh?" from Boxer in return.

"Nothing," he said. "No response?"

"Nope. I'm going to try some other frequencies."

"Roger. Keep up the active scan; focus it toward the jump point. I don't want to be surprised by someone else coming through."

"Never stopped."

Good. And Jason had expected Boxer would do that; he'd been in the game just as long as Jason had, and knew his stuff.

Still, a little watchteam backup never hurt anyone.

The skiff drew nearer to the intruder over the next several minutes without any response to Boxer's hails, and the image in the data window became more clear. Jason found he had to work to tear his eyes away from it to do his normal instrument scan and take care of his piloting duties.

Not that it was particularly interesting to look at, in and of itself. The design wasn't exactly novel, except for the wings, which were useless in a pure spaceship. But it was fascinating, nevertheless. The mystery, yes, but also the possibilities.

Was this a new Dominance ship? Or someone else, who had come through Dominance space to the Confederation?

That opened all manner of potentials that sent Jason into speculation for a long several minutes before he noticed...

The wingtip running lights and the white dorsal lights on the intruder were flickering.

Wait. No, not flickering, like the power was failing. Blinking. Blinking rhythmically, almost intentionally.

Jason blinked, and focused in on the lights. The pattern was vaguely familiar. Like something he'd seen once...

He drew in a quick breath. "Boxer, the contact's lights, I think they're blinking in Morse Code!"

"What?" A pause, then, "Hey you're right. I think. I don't remember my Morse very well. Do you?"

Jason shook his head before he recalled Boxer couldn't see him. "I remember SOS, that's about it. Are you recording video or just stills?"

"Both, and I'm way ahead of you. Sending the video feed to HATHERLY now. They can have the comms techs decode it."

"Outstanding."

Jason glanced at the contact data on his piloting bubble again. Time to intercept had ticked down to less than fifteen minutes. Hopefully HATHERLY would be able to make something out of the intruder's message—if it actually was one—before then. Otherwise things might get awkward.

The timer was down to less than five minutes, and the vessel was visible to the naked eye through his piloting bubble, when the call came.

"Lobo Six Zero Seven, this is HATHERLY Actual, over."

Jason blinked, and heard Boxer draw in a surprised breath. The CO himself was on the line? This was about to get heavy. He keyed his ship-to-ship comms control, which was set to HATHERLY's frequency. "Lobo Six Zero Seven."

"Six Zero Seven, we've decoded most of their message. They say they can receive but their transmitter is damaged. They claim to be a transport of the Free Republic of Hazador Navy, and they have three members of their Parliament onboard. They are fleeing Dominance aggression and have requested asylum and protection, over."

The Free what of what? "Roger. Interrogative: Free Republic of Hazador?"

"We don't know either, Six Zero Seven. But whoever they are, if the Dominance is hostile to them they are potential allies for us. I am granting them asylum pending official word back from Admiral Kennerly at System HQ. That will take at least 2 hours. In the meantime, we are preparing the VBSS team to rendezvous with the contact and extract its personnel. Your orders are to take up station between the contact and the jump point, monitor the situation, and if necessary defend the contact against Dominance attack, if they should come through the jump point. Over."

Defend them? With what? The skiffs *could* be loaded out with a light anti-ship strike package, but Jason's wasn't; he had the surveillance and reconnaissance package. Both of the skiffs based on HATHERLY did. He had a light plasma cannon for self defense—not good for much more than scaring a small civilian pleasure craft—and his countermeasures system, which *hopefully* could spoof incoming torpedoes or missiles aimed at his skiff. Maybe.

And that was it.

"Roger."

He couldn't keep the doubt out of his voice, and suspected it transmitted through the comms circuit.

A moment later, the CO's reply confirmed it. "We are refitting Six Zero Eight to a strike package. ETA for launch 35 minutes. HATHERLY will be in weapons range in one hour. Until then you're it. Do your best, Six Zero Seven, over."

It took a moment for what the CO said to sink in. He knew their limitations, that they likely couldn't do much except soak up a missile or two. And that's what he expected them to do, if necessary.

Yeah, it got real heavy. Real heavy, real fast.

"Roger."

"Good luck, gentlemen. HATHERLY out."

Jason blew out a long, slow breath.

"Well that sucks," Boxer said, and Jason's long exhale became a laugh that was part tension release, part resignation, and part legit humor of the deadpan way he said it.

"Yeah, it does."

"Mom told me to become a dentist. Guess I shoulda listened to her."

Jason laughed again, 75% humor this time. "Well, too late for that. We're here so let's get it done."

It only took a few minutes to get positioned as the CO ordered. Jason put the skiff about a kilometer away from the contact and rotated the skiff so the countermeasure system's antennas and decoy launchers were oriented directly toward the jump point.

If they were going to do this, better give themselves the best chance possible.

Then there wasn't much to do but sit back and wait. And take a better look at the contact. This close, Jason could tell his initial estimate of the vessel's size was wrong; it was about three times the size of the skiff, and he could see a number of small portholes running down the sides of the hull: windows for the important travelers to look out from their cabins, unless he missed his guess.

He wondered what they were up to, over there. HATHERLY had taken over comms with them, and told them their request for asylum was granted and to expect the VBSS team's arrival within two hours. They probably had all sorts of great entertainment equipment onboard to pass the time.

He found himself envying them that.

"Shoulda brought a deck of cards," Jason said, and Boxer laughed.

"I'm always down to take your money," the SASO said, and Jason snorted.

"I was thinking Go Fish, not Poker."

"Coward."

Jason snorted again, then looked at his chronometer. From what the CO said, Jerky and Hobo should be launching in another 10 minutes, and HATHERLY would be in weapons range in 35.

He willed the minutes to tick by more quickly, and it seemed to be working.

Eight minutes now.

Five.

"Maybe we'll get lucky, and they won't bother to continue the—" Boxer cut off abruptly, then said, "Aw hell. Gravitics just pegged again."

The way the skiff was oriented, Jason couldn't see the jump gate's rainbow display this time. All the same, there was no doubt what had just happened, and his spirits, which had been rising by the minute almost without his noticing it, dropped down into his boots.

"Crap," he said.

"New contact. Correction, two new contacts. They're actively scanning. From their transmissions looks like a Dominance Frigate and Corvette."

"Double crap."

"That's the truth," Boxer said. Then the tension in his voice ratcheted up to 11. "I'm reading fire control radars now. Locking on us."

"Rig for combat," Jason said, and it was like the words flipped a switch in his mind. His thoughts crystalized, resolving down into the checklist of things to do, and he began going down it.

Reactor to max power. Engine limiters off. Plasma cannon safety off—it might matter.

He flipped a switch on the left hand side of his pilot's chair, and heard the hatch between himself and Boxer slide shut.

Then he reached up and pulled on the padded collar of his flight suit. The flexible plasteel hood that was contained within the padding released, and he pulled it over his head. A practiced run of his hands along the seam of the hood activated the adhesive there, and he secured to the rest of his flight suit. A hose connection from the skiff's atmosphere system to a fitting on his suit and he had airflow, and his flight suit was now space ready.

"You set, Boxer?"

"Affirm."

"Ok." Jason drew a breath and steeled himself. "Commence jamming. Decoys ready?"

"Jammers on. Decoys good to go."

The implants in Jason's right ear crackled, then a new voice came over his comms circuit. Jason recognized Jerky immediately.

"Lobo Six Zero Seven, this is Six Zero Eight. We're off, doing max burn to you. ETA ten minutes. Weapons range in five."

Jason looked at the chronometer. They got out ahead of schedule—awesome. "Roger. We've got it covered until then. We drifted far enough from the jump gate they won't be able to split up and gain enough bearing separation to come at us from different axes for at least a few minutes, over."

There was a noticeable hesitation before Jerky replied, "Roger. We're going to come on your starboard side. HATHERLY is maneuvering to come in from below and to port."

Good to know. "Roger, out," he said, just as he heard in the left implant a deep voice speaking heavily-accented but smooth English.

"This is the Tsago Dominace warship YANGTZE to Icaran

Confederation vessel. We are here to apprehend Dominance subjects who are fugitives from justice. You are directed to cease your jamming immediately and stand aside. Failure to dc so will be regarded as an act of aggression against the Tsago Dominance, requiring an immediate and overwhelming response."

Well this was going downhill fast. Jason opened his mouth to reply and brought his thumb down onto the transmit control button.

Then stopped as HATHERLY beat him to it.

"This is the Icaran Confederation Navy Cruiser HATHERLY to Dominance warships. Your presence here uninvited is a violation of Confederation territory. The Free Republic of Hazador Navy vessel is under our protection. You will cease your pursuit and depart this system immediately. Failure to comply or any further aggressive action from you, will be viewed as an act of war against the Icaran Confederation."

Silence over the comms circuits followed, punctuated only by a loud thumping in Jason's ears. He wasn't sure whether it was the drum line from the music Boxer still had playing over their internal comms circuit or the pounding of his heart. Or both.

"They still locked on us?" he asked, and was amazed that his voice came out steady and strong.

"Fire control radar is still up, yes. Hopefully the jamming broke their lock."

Yeah. Hopefully.

Finally, the Dominance voice came back on the circuit. "This is an internal Dominance matter, HATHERLY. You have no right to interfere."

"You are in Confederation territory, YANGTZE. Depart now, or we will consider your vessels hostile."

And that had to give the Dominance commander pause. He had two ships, yes. But a Frigate and a Corvette.

HATHERLY was a brand spanking new top-of-the line battle-cruiser, fresh from post-delivery overhaul and upgrades, with the latest and greatest in ICN technology and weaponry. She outgunned the two Dominance ships by at least 4 to 1 all by herself.

They had to know that.

But they also had to know she was still pretty far away. Did they have good intel on ICN weapons engagement ranges for the latest hardware?

Jason said a quick prayer that if they did have any intel, it overstated those ranges.

Because if they knew they still had 20 minutes until HATHERLY could do anything to them...that was plenty of time to blow him up.

Jerky and Hobo would return fire, naturally. And their strike package could certainly do some damage, especially to the Corvette.

But that wouldn't help him and Boxer very much.

So he sweated by the seconds that passed after HATHER-LY's response. Naturally, the band's male singer decided to engage in a particularly guttural and brutal chorus, accompanied by a guitar riff that sounded like it could kill a platoon at 100 yards by itself.

All of a sudden Jason really wished for some nice opera music instead.

More seconds passed, but they seemed to stretch like years. Then the Dominance officer spoke again.

"This insult to the Dominance will not be forgotten, HATHERLY. Or forgiven. YANGTZE out."

Ok...what did that mean?

From the way he had aligned the skiff he couldn't see the Dominance warships' icons on his piloting bubble directly; they were just over his right shoulder, past the extent of the plasteel bubble. There was just a pair of red arrowheads pointing in that direction, telling him hostile contacts were in that direction.

He got the strong urge to yaw the skiff around so he could see better. But that might bring the jammers and decoy launchers out of optimal alignment, and that would be bad.

So he'd just have to suck up having an incomplete picture.

Boxer, of course, would have a more clear view on his SASO tactical display, and just then Jason envied him his position, even though he never got to fly.

But only for a second.

Then both red arrowheads winked out and Boxer gave a little whoop.

"Jump point opened again. They bugged out."

Jason let out a breath he hadn't even realized he had been holding and sagged back into his seat, relief flooding through him.

He looked down at his hands and realized they were shaking. That had been close. Damn close.

Jerky's voice came over the comms circuit again. "We're in range, Six Zero Seven."

Jason barked out a quick laugh. Just in the nick of time!

But into the comms circuit he said, "Roger. Break. HATHERLY this is Lobo Six Zero Seven. Dominance warships have departed the system and Six Zero Eight is on station. Six Zero Seven is RTB."

The CO's voice came over the circuit again. "This is HATHERLY Actual. Come on home. Well done, gentlemen. We'll take it from here."

"Roger. Six Zero Seven out." Then over the internal comms circuit he said, "I dunno about you, but I need a beer."

"Or six," Boxer said. "Think the CO will let us have an advance on a few days' rations?"

"Doubt it."

"Yeah you're probably right. Countermeasures system secured. De-rigging for combat. Let's go home."

Jason nodded emphatic agreement, and spun the skiff around onto an intercept course for HATHERLY. Then he advanced the throttle and they hurtled forward toward home base, the hangar, a beer, and his rack.

As they passed the strange ship that had made their last couple of hours so interesting, he hoped it would all end up being worth it.

Then he shrugged. He'd probably never know.

SPIRIT FORECLOSURE

At the beginning of the year, I participated in a writing workshop which taught how to write fantasy caper stories. Over the
course of that workshop, one of the assignments was to write a
caper in a modern setting that incorporated fantasy elements.

This is that story, and it was super fun to write.

Enjoy!

I t was one of those formal occasions that Sylvie normally
hated.

A large ballroom on the mezzanine level of the Penin-
sula Hotel downtown—which made it a pain in the neck to get
to in the first place—with twenty-foot ceilings boasting crown
molding that was designed to look hand-carved but was probably prefab.

Half a dozen crystal chandeliers lent a soft white glow that
combined with the pale beige of the walls to make the place
seem warm despite the AC being set just a tad too low.

There was plush red and blue carpeting on the floors, and
formal dining tables for eight scattered all over in front of the
long, raised VIP table and lectern set opposite the entrance.

Bars stocked with top-shelf wine and liquor bottles stood in
each of the room's corners.

And everywhere, men in tuxedos that stood out in their
uniformity and women in evening gowns that varied from styl-
ishly tasteful to slightly above hooker-tier in their slinkiness.

A string quartet played off to the right, Bach unless Sylvie
missed her guess, just loud enough to be heard over the general
din of hundreds of conversations taking place all at once.

Off to the left of the VIP table stood a large display placard
with gold text on a black background that read, "Twenty-
Second Annual Humanitarian of the Year Awards," above a
portrait of the Guest of Honor, Terrence Manahan, plump-
faced and grey-haired, with a smug, self-satisfied smile on his
face staring out at the crowd.

The room smelled of various women's perfumes—flowery
and subtle and musky and hit-you-over-the-head-with-lavender
—and the occasional aftershave from the men, and the subtle
odor of steak and chicken wafting from the tables from the meal
the wait staff was just finishing up serving.

Torture. But necessary for this night's work.

Sylvie stepped inside, her feet already aching from the dark blue pumps she had forced them into earlier. The silky smoothness of her evening gown—dark blue to match her pumps, ankle-length, with spaghetti straps and a neckline that plunged just enough to hint at her cleavage—offset that discomfort, but just barely and not enough to stop her longing for her usual sneakers and yoga pants.

But again, necessary tonight.

Beside her, Jeremy gave her a wry sidelong look, his grey-green eyes flashing with a mixture of pity and amusement beneath his roguishly-combed red-brown hair. "Suck it up," he didn't say, though she could feel it wafting from him.

"Shut up," she said under her breath, and he chuckled.

"Just be glad we don't have to be here all night," he said softly in his rich baritone. He looked around quickly, then focused in on the bar setup to their right, where a perky-looking blonde in the pseudo-tux of the wait staff stood holding court over her liquor domain. "I'll get us some drinks. Go do your thing."

He didn't wait for her reply but strode briskly toward the bar. And the bartender. No doubt he had more than drinks in mind.

And for a moment, as she watched his efficient, almost elegant stride and the way his shoulders filled out his tux jacket, she almost envied the girl.

Almost.

She knew better than to let him in that way, though. And anyway, she had her own target in mind.

As she wove her way past the tables for the rank-and-file toward the VIP area, tides of feeling ebbed and flowed over her, the "gift" of her lineage.

Jealousy from a mid-40s brunette as she stared at her husband who was spending far too much time talking to the

20-something blonde sitting next to him. Frustration bordering on anger from a waiter who stalked past her on his way about his duties. Embarrassment from a teenager standing with his father talking to a woman who was far too old to be wearing a dress that practically flopped her boobs out, as he squirmed to try to mask his body's reaction to the sight. The older woman's satisfaction that she could still have that effect on a male, even—especially?—one who was far too young for her.

Those and dozens more, the inner feelings of each and every person she passed. Sylvie squirmed within herself as she picked up the pace, battling to ignore the feelings, keep focused on the task at hand.

This was why she hated these sorts of large gatherings—any large gatherings, really. Too hard to filter the feelings out.

Inwardly, she thanked her lucky stars she had only the empathic "gift". Others of the spirit-touched were full-on telepaths; that would have been hell on earth.

For a moment she questioned the wisdom of agreeing to this job. A large part of her screamed to get out of there. Go someplace quiet, where she wouldn't be accosted by so many, from all sides.

She shoved that down. Hard. She was here. Now get the job done.

Behind the lectern, higher up on the wall, was a large screen for displaying presentations. From their earlier scouting, the computer controlling it was to the left, behind the display placard where the guy running the show could work without being seen by the crowd.

And yes, as she rounded yet another of the dining tables and got an angle on the placard she could see it. And the presentation guy, at work making his final preparations.

Sylvie smiled with anticipation. "Got him," she said.

In the earpiece hidden away inside her left ear she heard Russ' voice. "All set here."

She moved in for the kill.

Three Weeks Earlier

When Sylvie answered the knock on her door, she wasn't surprised to see Jeremy. He hadn't come around in months, but somehow it seemed perfectly natural that he would show up on a Sunday afternoon, smiling that winning smile of his.

He was in khaki cargo pants and a navy-blue polo shirt, and he had a Starbucks cup in each hand.

"Hey Sylvie," he said, and held the one in his left hand out to her.

Even without the feeling of cautious purpose seeping off of him, she would have immediately been on her guard, no matter how natural it seemed for him to be there.

"Jeremy," she said, and caught herself adjusting the loose PINK t-shirt she wore so it would settle better on her shoulders. That almost automatic reaction to his frank gaze just made her distrust go all the higher. "Been a while."

"Too long, so I figured I'd see what my favorite spirit-touched girl's been up to."

She snorted and snatched the coffee cup out of his hand, then turned back into her little apartment and its smaller living room/entryway.

His sense shifted from cautious purpose to almost genuine curiosity for a second as he followed her inside and looked around at her black leather couch, which showed many more creases from wear than the last time he had been here, and the glass-topped coffee table in front of it. And in particular the empty bottle of Jameson and trio of shot glasses sitting in the middle of it.

"Hard night last night?"

Sylvie shrugged and settled down into her matching leather stuffed chair and took a sip of her coffee. He got it right, as always: French roast with just the right amount of cream, no sugar.

"What do you want, Jeremy?"

"Can't a guy catch up with an old pal?"

She raised an eyebrow, ignoring the completely feigned look of hurt on his face; his emotions hadn't changed at all, except for a hint of amusement that barely touched the purpose that dominated him.

He returned her gaze for a moment, then shrugged and sat down on the edge of her couch. He placed his own coffee cup down on the table without drinking. "I've got a job."

"You usually do."

Jeremy flashed a quick grin. "Simple scam, but it needs someone with your talents. You available?"

"Could be. What is it?"

"It's a real Robin Hood bit; you'll love it. Hotshot real estate guy who's been scamming the little folk." He raised an eyebrow. "He scammed the wrong guy though, and we're going to make him pay."

A shiver ran up Sylvie's spine, and for a moment she wasn't in her living room talking with Jeremy anymore. She was eight, watching her mother sob uncontrollably on her father's shoulder as they drove away from their home in a cab, not understanding why Dad said they could never go back.

The look of devastation on his face even while he was trying to console Mom.

She was starting to clench her fists. The resistance of the

Starbucks cup against her hand's pressure snapped her back to reality, and she gave herself a little shake.

Moving slowly, carefully, she set the cup down atop the coffee table, then looked back up at Jeremy, carefully smoothing her face to neutral. But she could see in his eyes, feel from his emotions, that he had noticed, and knew his words had the effect he wanted on her.

She knew it too; it almost didn't matter who the target was, she was in, and she knew it.

They both did.

"Who?"

Jeremy grinned broadly, the grin of a predator who smelled unsuspecting prey, and raised his other eyebrow to join the first.

They met to make their preparations in the same place as the last scam Sylvie had done with Jeremy: a conference room in the McMillan Building. It was one of those places that rents office and meeting spaces to businesses that either don't need or can't afford to maintain permanent spaces.

Jeremy had a phony business that he used to rent the spot: Dimension Concepts, Inc. Or maybe it was real; Sylvie didn't know for sure, and didn't really care.

Regardless, it made for much nicer digs than most other crews she'd worked with used. The conference room could have belonged to a Fortune 500 company: all mahogany table and hardwood floors, a big LCD flat-screen on the wall and teleconference gear at each spot at the table. A computer terminal at a small desk next to the screen to control the teleconference gear or run presentations. Tasteful landscape paintings on the walls. The faint scent of pine on the air from an air freshener somewhere.

Much, much nicer than her usual.

She recognized one of the two men in the room when she and Jeremy arrived.

Russ was a short, skinny, mousy-looking guy in his early 30s who was already fully grey and starting to go bald. You wouldn't figure him for a tough guy, but she happened to know he was a champion amateur MMA fighter. A welterweight, but still.

You *would* figure him for an IT guy though, and surprise... he was. He was sitting at the conference room's computer, typing away doing something in a red and blue plaid flannel shirt and jeans, his wire-rimmed glasses low on his nose.

When she entered, he looked over, saw her, and smiled broadly. "Hey Syl. Long time no see." He gave off strong waves of friendly affection, and beneath it a more carnal desire that flashed and then almost immediately crumpled. She assumed he suppressed it by the discipline that made him a champion fighter; he certainly had never tried to make a pass at her.

Wise of him.

"How've you been, Russ?"

He shrugged. "Same ol', same ol'. You know how it is. What—"

"You didn't say anything about having a spirit-touched on the crew."

Sylvie looked over at the stranger, sitting at the center seat on the opposite side of the conference table from the entrance. Asian, from his bone structure Korean unless she was very off base. Average height, muscular, not bad-looking, in a white, collared shirt that had the top two buttons open. He wore a silver watch on his left wrist and kept his hair closely cropped, and he was looking at her with eyes that didn't even begin to express the waves of distrust that flooded off him.

It wasn't the first time someone had reacted to her lineage that way, but Sylvie found herself impressed, actually. Some spirit-touched traits showed plainly for all to see. Hers were easier to miss: a very slight pointing to her ears, the faintest of silver tinting to her skin. Most people didn't notice at all.

He had plainly had more interaction with her "kind" than the vast majority of the populace.

Russ scowled over at him. "Calm down, Vic. It's not like she's a vampire."

Vic returned the scowl. "Vampires aren't real."

Sylvie put on a well-practiced, secretive little smile. "Are you sure about that?" She pitched her tone carefully, inflections that she knew from a lifetime of absorbing the emotions and fears of those around her would trigger his fear response.

It worked. Better than she thought it would.

He gave a jerk, almost pushing his seat back from the table he recoiled so hard, and his eyes went from merely distrustful to suddenly terrified, this time accurately mimicking the emotions within him.

Beside her, Jeremy cleared his throat loudly. "That's enough." From the corner of her eye she saw he was giving her a hard, no-nonsense stare. He knew exactly what she had done, and his expression screamed that he would not tolerate it. The sharp focus, the feeling of determined command flowing from him confirmed it.

She returned his look and nodded, then let out a slow breath and looked back at Vic. She made a little apologetic shrug of her shoulders.

"Vic, this is Sylvie," Jeremy said, still eyeing her for a moment. "I've worked with her for years, and yes, she's on the team." He turned his commanding gaze back to Vic. "If that's a problem for you, you can go, and we'll get someone else to do your part."

Vic's immediate fear response was fading, replaced by affront combined with what only be called professional assurance as he returned Jeremy's look and snorted. "No one else is as good as I am." His eyes flicked back toward Sylvie for a second. "I don't like the idea of someone poking around in my head."

"If it makes you feel any better," Sylvie said in a normal, conversational tone, "I'm not a telepath. I can sense your emotions, that's all."

"So much better," he said, sarcasm dripping from his voice.

Jeremy gestured toward the entrance. "There's the door."

Desire to be gone fought with something else within Vic. Professional pride? He stewed back and forth for a few seconds, then blew out a breath and nodded. "If you trust her, fine. I'm in." He looked at her again. "Just stay out of my head."

"No problem with that."

Silence lingered for another couple seconds as Jeremy just stared at Vic. Finally, he returned the nod. "Ok." He looked back at Sylvie. "Sylvie, Vic has a PhD in quantitative mathematics. He worked on Wall Street for ten years and used to moonlight as a researcher for the Federal Reserve."

"Still do, actually," Vic said, and Jeremy raised an eyebrow, surprise flooding through him momentarily before he went back to his calm feeling of command.

"And he's right," Jeremy went on. "You won't find a better finance and money guy anywhere in this country."

Wow. What was a guy like that doing in this business...? Then Sylvie remembered Enron, Bernie Maddoff, Ponzi, and half a dozen others, and it made sense.

"Nice to meet you," she said, putting on a conciliatory expression and the tone to match.

He just nodded silently in response.

"Well." Jeremy looked at Russ. "All set?"

Russ nodded, and Jeremy took the seat at the head of the

table, facing the LCD screen, and gestured for Sylvie to sit as well. She took the seat directly across from Vic.

The lights lowered and the screen turned on, and Russ entered a keystroke on the computer. A picture came up of a man in his 50s, plump but in the way that said he used to be in very good shape not so very long ago. He wore a navy blue pinstriped suit and a red power tie, and was mid-stride down a city street with a black briefcase in his hand.

"The mark is Terrence Manahan. He's basically the king of local real estate financing, and he's made a living screwing over the people who borrowed from him for decades, while making the world think he's a good guy."

"So he's just like everyone else in the business," Vic said.

"Pretty much," Jeremy agreed. "Two months ago he used loopholes in the fine print of his mortgages to foreclose on two dozen families."

From Russ, Sylvie sensed affront that almost but not quite matched her own; though hers was buried beneath a deeper remembered pain that she had to work hard not to let show.

From Vic, detached, professional curiosity. A hint of admiration?

She hadn't truly taken offense to his earlier reaction to her. But now she found herself actively disliking him. It was petty, born of her own feelings. No reason he should truly care. That didn't matter. He *should*.

"What Manahan didn't know is one of the families was the brother of one of the people at the accounting firm he contracts to handle his company's books, his wife, and their five children. Our client knows the ins and outs of Manahan's financial setup, and he wants payback for his brother."

"Understandable," Sylvie said, careful to keep her voice professionally neutral despite the continued turmoil within her.

Jeremy nodded.

"How much is our client paying us?" Vic asked.

"Nothing."

Vic opened his mouth, but Jeremy walked over what he was about to say.

"Manahan will be. In three weeks he closes a one hundred million dollar deal to purchase residential and commercial real estate in three states. He's got partners and financing lined up, and when he pushes send on the payment we're going to intercept and divert it to where we want it to go."

Vic pursed his lips. "And where is that?"

"GLAAD, Greenpeace, a fund to reimburse the affected families. And us, of course. Ten percent, split four ways. Do the math."

"I take it he's a Republican," Russ said.

"And puts on airs of being a Christian. Where else *should* he be donating, am I right?" Jeremy couldn't keep the anticipatory amusement from his voice.

Chuckles all around, Sylvie included. Made sense to her.

"So what's the catch?" Vic said.

"There can be no link leading back to our client, or the accounting firm. It has to look like Manahan did this himself." Jeremy looked at Vic. "And of course the money can't be traceable to any of us, or the families."

Vic nodded slowly. "I can think of a few ways to accomplish that. Could get complicated though. It would help if I had direct access to the company's finance system."

"Thought you'd say that. And that's the rub." He looked at Sylvie. "You'll have to get us inside."

"Daytime or at night?"

Jeremy shrugged. "Maybe both. Russ and I have done a bit of scouting though, and I think we've found a way in." He grinned at her. "He's just your type."

The image on the screen shifted to a young man—early

20s tops—sitting at a table in a mall's food court. He had scruffy brown hair and a little dusting of a mustache. He was sipping on a fountain drink through a straw and had on a white, short-sleeved collared shirt that screamed "Nerd" from the mouths of the trio of pens he had stuck into the breast pocket. His eyes had a far-away look like he wasn't focused on his surroundings.

Sylvie rolled her eyes slightly. Not her type at all. But probably perfect, all the same. "Let me guess." She gave Russ a teasing little grin. "He's an IT guy."

Russ returned the grin with one of his own. "Bingo. On-site tech support, works directly for Manahan's CIO. Name's Thomas Bilinger. And as you can imagine, he's lonely."

The next screen showed multiple profiles from basically all the online dating apps, including several Sylvie had never heard of. All Bilinger, and not a one of them worthy of a second glance.

Poor Thomas did *not* know how to present an appealing case.

"So it's charm poor Tommy and get him to do...what?"

Russ leaned forward in his chair. "It can't look like an outside breach; it has to originate within Manahan's organization. So we'll need admin-level access to their system, and in particular the finance side. We need to get his login credentials," he pointed at Bilinger.

Sylvie frowned. "But that will make it look like he did it, not Manahan."

Russ blinked, then returned the frown.

Jeremy nodded. "Good point."

After a few seconds of silence as they pondered, Vic snorted. "So just find a different admin account. They must have a generic login. Or get him to make one. Then once you're in on that account, change Manahan's password. Then we do what we do and you use the admin account to change it back again."

Russ blinked again, then chuckled. "I suppose that could work..." But he sounded doubtful.

"One thing at a time," Jeremy said. "Sylvie, you and Russ get cracking on young Tommy here. Figure out what the best way to go is, and we'll meet back here in a couple days."

Vic said, "And I'll get started lining up the transactions." He pursed his lips. "This could be fun."

The hardest part about linking up with Tommy was deciding which of Sylvie's five Tinder accounts to use. In the end, she decided on Sarah, the pretty and friendly legal secretary who was looking for a smart, reliable, nice guy because she was fed up with all the jerks out there.

Every nice guy's fantasy that never pans out.

A couple DMs later they were in a Starbucks. She with her French roast, he with some frothy frapa-something-or-other.

It was easier than she thought it would be. He really was terribly lonely; it wafted from him in waves that would swamp the Titanic. And he also really, really liked her.

Part of her felt sorry for him.

"Wow, that's really interesting," she said, in tones that would make him feel it was genuine without pushing over into the realm of flattery.

He nodded emphatically. "Yeah, we're doing it right." He leaned forward over his cup, eagerness to share—to impress—spilling out of him. "Some places talk a good game about protecting client data. But they all get hacked and their people get doxed." He put on a smug smile. "Can't happen with us."

She made an exaggerated shudder. "Yeah, a couple years

ago we had a disgruntled former client who managed to hack into our database. Trying to get his money back I guess?" She shook her head. "Some confidential information got stolen, and the partners went into a tizzy about it."

Tommy shook his head sympathetically. "Did they catch him?"

She nodded. "He's doing fifteen years, I hear."

"Serves him right. But you really needed one of these." He fished in his pocket and pulled out a key ring. Three keys on it: a Volkswagen, a bicycle lock, and probably his front door. There was also a rectangular black hunk of plastic with a little screen on one side next to three buttons.

Sylvie blinked. "What is that?" She didn't have to fake her intonation to show curiosity; this time it was genuine.

"You know about Two Factor Authentication."

She nodded. "I hate that. Every stupid app wants to send me a code on my phone. It's very annoying. And what if I don't have my phone?" She made that especially plaintive, helpless almost.

Tommy nodded. "Yeah, lots of issues with that method. This," he held the piece of plastic up between them, "does the same thing without a phone."

He dug his fingernail into a notch on the side of the it, and a USB plug flipped out. "You log in with your password, then when the computer prompts you, you plug this in," he pointed at the little screen and buttons, "Enter your PIN code, and then you're in." Tommy grinned. "It's encrypted so it can't be hacked, and it identifies you individually so the system knows you're a legitimate login."

"Wow." She reached out, and Tommy let her take it.

Sylvie turned it over in her hand, examining it. The screen looked like a simple, old-school LCD. Probably only for showing numbers so low resolution. The two smaller buttons were labeled + and -, and the larger ENTER.

She handed it back to him. "So how would you enter your PIN code? With those buttons?" She put a subtle emphasis, a twisting of the intonation, onto the "you" and "your," tuned to appeal to his desire to impress, and his self-satisfaction.

This part was always tricky, but if she got it just...right...

His eyes lit up. "Want to see?"

She nodded, and he bent over to the laptop bag he had set down next to his chair when they sat. He came back up with an HP laptop, scooted his chair around the table so he was caddy-corner to her, then opened it up.

"It's like this," he said, and went through the process he had just described. She watched carefully. He typed too quickly for her to catch all his password, but it was seven keystrokes containing Q, 8, and lower-case L.

But the LCD on the 2FA device did indeed show his pin code as he entered it.

2-6-1-8-9

"Wow, that *is* really easy."

He nodded. "And effective." He waggled a finger at her. "You should tell your partners about it. Maybe you'll get a bonus."

Sylvie giggled softly. "Oh I doubt that. They're tight when it comes to money."

Tommy rolled his eyes and gave a little snort. "Tell me about it. My boss..." He shook his head. "You know he has a separate 2FA fob for financial transactions?"

Sylvie blinked. "Seriously?"

"Yeah. Guess he doesn't trust us or something. Mr. Manahan himself has to approve transactions over a certain amount. So you can imagine the Christmas bonuses are not exactly huge."

A certain amount of bitterness crept into Tommy's voice when he said that, but he was feeling anxiety. Deep anxiety. And disappointment.

Like he needed money, and had thought the bonus would set him up and then he got let down. Hard.

"That sucks," she said, and slipped her hand overtop his, giving it a gentle squeeze for a second.

He blinked, surprise followed by pleasure flooding through him at her touch.

"So he's carrying two of those things on his key chain? That's starting to get bulky."

Tommy frowned slightly, then shook his head. "Nah, I think he keeps it in a safe somewhere in his office. No need to bring it home, right?"

Right.

* * *

"That is a big problem." Russ looked and sounded grim. He felt worse, almost hopeless.

They were back in the conference room, and Sylvie had just given the rest of the team the run-down on her time with Tommy.

"There must be a way around it," Jeremy said.

Russ shook his head. "No, these sorts of setups are solid. The fobs are usually SHA-256 encrypted so forget hacking it. Unless we actually had Manahan's fob and PIN code, we're out of luck."

Silence around the room as everyone pondered that. Frowns also.

Vic blew out a breath. "Well that sucks. I've got a great setup for the money." He shook his head. "Hate to let it go to waste."

Jeremy perked up a bit. "What is it?"

"Well from the info the accountant gave you, the funds will be transferred from three of Manahan's accounts. I plan to divert the money into six dummy accounts at banks in the Caymans. Then into four crypto exchanges. I'll convert from Bitcoin to Verge to Doge to Ripple to Ethereum then back to Bitcoin and into six separate Ledger wallet addresses. Then back to the crypto exchanges to convert to dollars. Then four different FOREX markets. We'll convert to Euro, then Rubles, then Yuan, then to Swiss Francs. Separate accounts for each transfer, of course." He drew a breath. "Then I'll send it all into several numbered Swiss accounts. We can make dispersals anonymously from there."

Sylvie blinked. Twice.

"That's...a lot," she said.

Vic shrugged. "It's a lot of money." He grinned. "And I'm pretty sure I can work the arbitrage to make a profit off the whole thing, too."

Jeremy chuckled. "Of course you will. And how will we justify the payouts to the families?"

Another shrug. "Don't pay them. More for us."

In any other circumstance Sylvie could relate and agree. But eight year old her screamed that was unacceptable.

Vic noticed her glare and cocked an eyebrow at her. "What?"

Jeremy spoke before she could. "No, the deal with our client is they get made whole. Find a non-profit, a goodwill donation center, something. Some excuse to get them the money without it biting them or us in the ass."

Vic frowned, looking hard at Jeremy for a moment. Then he shrugged again. "Fine. But it'll have to be spread out over time. It's easier to justify than a big lump sum all at once."

"Whatever. Just figure out a way." He looked back at Russ.

"Assuming we can even get the money to begin with. Russ, there's really nothing we can do with this fob thing?"

Russ spread his hands helplessly. "I can't hack it. Can you figure a way to get Manahan's code?"

Jeremy was silent for a long couple seconds. "No."

"Then I don't know what to tell you."

A thought occurred to Sylvie. "Hold on a second. These fobs. They're what, a flash drive with some encryption on it that's code activated?"

"Not really, but the analogy is close."

"So how much storage space is on them?"

"It doesn't really work like that. It's—" He stopped, and she could see the wheels turning in his head. Sudden excitement, tempered with caution bloomed within him. "Sylvie did you see the model of the fob, who makes it?"

She frowned, thought, the shook her head.

"Well there's only a few companies that make things like that. If I can get my hands on one, and verify what I'm thinking... There may be a way after all."

"Oh?" Jeremy leaned forward in his chair. "How?"

"Let me and Sylvie work on it. I'll get back to you in a couple days."

Sylvie felt pretty satisfied when she sat back down at the conference table two days later.

Russ was streaming satisfaction like the sun.

Jeremy looked at the two of them with a weird expression on his face. His emotions showed curiosity but also, confusion.

"You two look like you won the lottery or something."

"We pretty much did," Russ said. "I ran Sylvie through the models on the market and she was able to identify the fob

Manahan uses. Then I went and picked up one." He reached into his pocket and pulled out the exact duplicate of the thing Tommy had shown her in Starbucks.

"Ok," Jeremy said, his tone saying, "Get on with it."

Russ grinned. "It's not a hard drive, per say, but there *is* information stored on it. The SHA-256 algorithm mostly. But there is a small ROM section holding a rudimentary operating system, for the user interface and some other technical things. Now," he leaned forward in his chair, "I'm pretty sure I can access that ROM and add a little bit of extra code."

Jeremy's eyebrows rose, and Vic perked up. He felt intrigued now.

Russ nodded. "A little virus, if you will. To trigger the transactions *we* want."

Jeremy opened his mouth, but Russ held up a hand to forestall him.

"It won't be a lot of code; there's not enough storage for that. Just a trigger. I'll have to plant the main virus code in Manahan's system, buried deep. Then when he puts the fob in and enters his PIN, the trigger activates the main virus, the transactions get changed and the money flies."

"So we'll need to get Manahan's fob, to modify it."

Russ nodded. "And we'll need access to his system." He turned to look at Sylvie. "You're going to have to get the rest of Tommy's password, and we'll need to borrow his fob."

Sylvie chewed it over for a moment. "I'm pretty sure I can get him to log in in front of me again." She grinned slyly. "He really, really wants to impress me."

"Don't we all," Jeremy said, drawing a short laugh from Russ. Vic cracked a tiny smile, but that was it. "So the way I see it," he raised his right hand and begin ticking off fingers, "Sylvie gets the password from him. Then we get his fob—at night while he's asleep is best I think—and break into Manahan's office.

Find his safe, crack it, and get his fob. Log in to the system and plant the virus. Plant the trigger on Manahan's fob. Then put everything back and watch the fireworks." He raised his eyebrows at Russ. "That about cover it?"

"Yep. Easy."

Sylvie snorted.

Jeremy sat back in his chair and looked over at Vic. "Figured out the families yet?"

Vic shrugged. "I think it's best if I open numbered accounts for each of them. Then we slip them the account information and let them do with it what they want. No traceable money changes hands, so no tax issue for them. If they go get the money from the accounts, it's not reported so, no tax issue in the future either."

"*If* they go," Sylvie said. "Most of them will assume it's a scam, like the Nigerian Prince thing."

Another shrug. "Not necessarily. I can make the notifications look very formal, professional, and they'll be able to contact the bank to verify the information if they choose. But I can't see any other way to get it to them without raising all sorts of flags. It's $500,000. I'll wager everyone will want to check it out at least. But if some choose to not accept..." He spread his hands.

He was feeling annoyed at Sylvie's objection, but also satisfied and sure of his conclusions, so Sylvie felt some of the wind taken from her sails.

Jeremy was frowning as he considered Vic's words for a moment. Then he nodded. "Ok, we'll do it that way." The frown turned upside down. "Well Sylvie, looks like you get to have another date with your boyfriend."

That did evoke laughs from everyone. Sylvie even allowed herself to join in.

Two weeks and three times meeting up with Tommy again, and Sylvie finally got the rest of his password.

6Q8feL#

Not at all complicated. Russ could have easily cracked it on his own, given enough time. And unlimited password attempts before the system would lock the user out. Sylvie was sure of that. But alas those conditions weren't in place, so she had to do it the in-person way.

Truth to tell, it wasn't nearly as unpleasant as many other scams she'd run over the years.

In fact, sitting across the table from him while they had dinner at a nice Italian place on the outskirts of downtown, she considered that he really wasn't all that bad a guy, really. He just needed some refining: develop more of a backbone. develop more muscles, and read something besides computer books.

Do that and he'd be fine for a girl.

Some other girl, not her. She didn't have the time or patience to mold him into what he should already be. And anyway, he was too young for her.

That didn't stop her from smiling—a nearly genuine smile— as they finished dinner and he got the bill.

"I'm interested to see your place," she said, and he paused in mid-signature on the credit card payment slip for the bill.

Surprise, then disbelief, then happiness and excitement. And arousal. But he kept it from showing on his face.

Mostly.

When he looked up to meet her eyes he almost appeared nonchalant. Calm. Sylvie was actually impressed by that.

"It's not far from here, actually," he said.

"Cool. Let's go."

He finished signing, then stood in a rush and held out his hand to her.

She took it, and they went.

"You weren't too hard on the boy I hope," Jeremy said as he worked the lock to Manahan's office.

He was down on his knees in front of the door, probing with his lock picks. Sylvie was behind one of the pillars out front of the building, keeping watch for wandering eyes. Or especially cops. Vic and Russ were in the car around the corner, waiting for the all-clear signal to follow them in once Jeremy got the door open.

Sylvie snorted out a chuckle. "He'll have a bit of a headache from the spike I put in his wine, but he'll be fine."

In her ear she heard Russ' voice, carried over their radios. "You tucked him in at least, I hope?"

"Of course. I'm not a barbarian. He'll wake up in bed with a glass of water, two aspirin, and a note from Sarah on his night-stand in the morning."

"Touching," Vic said dryly.

"Never let it be said Sylvie doesn't know how to take care of a man," Jeremy said, affectionate teasing in his emotions and in his voice both.

Sylvie sniffed but didn't reply. She couldn't help but smile slightly though.

Another couple minutes passed, then—

"And that's got it," Jeremy said. "We're in, gang."

Sylvie turned to see him holding the door open for her, his hand swinging in a "Come in, my lady," gesture that a doorman would make in an old movie.

She rolled her eyes, then hurried inside.

Manahan's personal office was all the way in back of the office spaces, to the left. It was smaller than she would have expected for a man who controlled as much wealth as he did. But it was done up nicely, even better than their rented conference space, if you could believe it.

The desk was massive. Mahogany for certain. The bookshelves on the wall to the desk's right were full. The stuffed leather seats to the left plump and comfy-looking. The painting of an elderly gentleman standing in front of bookshelves that looked remarkably like the ones on the wall opposite where the painting hung, with his hand in his pocket and the other holding a gold pocket watch while he stared out from the painting with and expression of utter confidence and command, was obviously old, and well-crafted.

Not shabby at all.

"If I were a safe, where would I be?" Jeremy asked as they walked into the place. Then he pointed at the painting. "Behind you."

And sure enough, the painting was mounted on a swivel, and as it turned out of the way it revealed a wall safe with a dial tumbler combination lock mounted in the wall behind it.

"How long's it been since you cracked a safe like that?" Sylvie asked.

Jeremy grinned at her. "Yesterday." He cracked his knuckles. "Only a few safe manufacturers that a guy like Manahan would go to. I've been practicing on all of the likely candidates for the last two weeks." Then he gave a jerk of his head toward the door, and she nodded.

His job was to crack the safe. Russ' job was to implant the viruses in the fob and on the network computer on Manahan's desk. Vic's job was to make sure Russ didn't screw up and get the account numbers wrong.

Her job was to keep a lookout.

So she went back to the front of the offices, to wait. And watch.

———

"Small change in plans," Jeremy said in the car.

He was driving Sylvie back to Tommy's place, to return his fob and keys. Russ and Vic had gotten out at the McMillan Building and gone their separate ways. But Sylvie had left her car back at the restaurant where she'd had dinner with Tommy. So Jeremy was giving her a lift.

"What do you mean?"

"When Russ was planting the virus in Manahan's computer, he found a hidden folder." He looked sidelong at Sylvie and raised an eyebrow. "His blackmail folder."

She blinked. "Blackmail?"

Jeremy nodded. "Bribes to officials. Records of dirty deals by competitors. Dirty deals that he ran for others' profit. Going back for years."

"Russ made a copy, I hope?"

"Oh yes. Client wants Manahan burned, so we're burning him. Money was going to be enough, but this will make it even better. And I know the perfect place to show it to the world." He grinned at her. "When's the last time you got dressed up?"

Sylvie groaned.

———

"Hi there."

The guy running the computer behind the display placard at the Humanitarian of the Year Awards looked up, saw Sylvie, did a double take, then grinned. "Can I help you, miss?"

"I just always get curious how these sorts of events work

behind the scenes. You're running the audio-visual show?"

The guy cocked an eyebrow at her. "Yeah. No DJ tonight so it's easy." His emotions said he enjoyed looking at her but was annoyed at the interruption of his work.

"What application do you use? Powerpoint, or…?"

The guy shook his head. "Depends what the presentation is and what the client needs. Look, I need to get back to work here, so if you don't mind?"

"Oh, I'm sorry." She pitched her tone to appeal to his sense of charity. "Have a great night." She turned to go.

Off to the left, emerging from one of the wait staff entrances, a short, skinny man with receding grey hair in the faux tux of the wait staff emerged and began walking toward the VIP stage.

"You too," said the audio-visual guy.

Sylvie met eyes with Russ, in the wait staff attire, and he nodded.

On queue, Sylvie turned her ankle and fell, crying out in surprise and pain that she did not feel.

The audio-visual guy rushed over. "All you alright, miss?" He crouched down beside her.

Behind him, Russ diverted from his course.

"I'm not sure," Sylvie said. "I think I twisted it maybe?"

Audio-visual guy winced and looked at her ankle. "It doesn't look swollen or anything. Do you mind if I—?" He gestured toward her foot.

Nodding, Sylvie extended her foot toward him.

Russ passed by the guy and reached his computer. Bending over quickly, he dipped his hand into his pocket then inserted a thumb drive into one of the computer's USB ports.

He'd told her it would take 15 seconds for the files on the drive to unpack and replace the presentation that had been loaded by Manahan's people earlier. Identical file names and everything.

Just had to keep audio-visual guy distracted for that time.

He touched her ankle, and she winced, saying "Ah!" like it hurt.

Audio-visual guy frowned. "Try moving it." He felt concern, but also annoyance. More annoyance over her continuing to interrupt him.

She slowly rolled her ankle around, making a little sniffle as it went through a full circle. Like it hurt but had full range of motion.

Behind audio-visual guy, Russ nodded at her, then pulled the thumb drive out.

Audio-visual guy shook his head. "Doesn't look like you have any issues moving it." He looked up to meet her eyes and gave a grin that was probably meant to be encouraging. "I think you'll be fine."

He straightened and held out his hand to help her up. Russ moved quickly behind him, going back toward the wait staff entrance he had just come through.

Sylvie accepted the help up, and took a minute to play-act testing putting her weight back onto her ankle. After a few seconds on it, she made to hobble around for a few steps, then righted herself and took a proper step, and grinned at him.

"You're right! Thank you. I'm so sorry to have been a hassle." She intoned the words to appeal to his vanity, his charity.

"No problem at all, miss. You have a good night, now."

She turned away, letting him get back to his duties, and smiled with satisfaction.

Jeremy was waiting at center stage, halfway between the entrance and the VIP stage, a champagne glass in each hand. When she reached him, he held out the one in his left, filled with golden bubbling fluid, to her.

She accepted, but didn't immediately drink. "Good to go," she said.

He nodded.

A few minutes later, a woman on the VIP stage stood and moved over to the lectern. She cleared her throat and said into the microphone, "Good evening, ladies and gentlemen."

All around the room, conversation ceased and people at the tables turned their heads to give the woman attention.

"I'm Sheila Easton, chair of the Humanitarian League. Welcome to our Twenty-Second Humanitarian Awards Banquet."

The crowd clapped politely, making quite a bit of noise considering how many of them there were, actually.

After a moment, the applause died down, and the woman spoke again. "This year we are honoring a man who needs no introduction, Terrence Manahan."

Another, shorter round of applause.

"Although he needs no introduction, we felt it was appropriate to make a short video about his career and the many great things he has done to merit this honor." She turned to the right and nodded toward where audio-visual guy was stationed.

The lights dimmed and the screen lit up. Then the video Jeremy and Russ had made over the last couple days began to play.

It started with a picture of Manahan, obviously drunk, on a beach somewhere surrounded by half a dozen bikini-clad girls half his age.

"Terrence Manahan is not who you think he is," said Jeremy's voice over the video. "He has made a career of graft, greed, and corruption. Observe."

Then followed the more lurid files that Russ had found on Manahan's computer. One after another after another. Videos of bribes. Records of forced foreclosures. On, and on.

Over by audio-visual guy's station, several tux-clad men had descended on the poor fellow. "Turn it off! Turn it off!" carried faintly to Sylvie's ears.

"I can't!" replied audio-visual guy, frantically.

"Manahan delights in stealing from people less powerful then him. Putting families on the street."

Another picture showed up, older than the others. Of a smiling, much younger Manahan in front of a house, as a stricken family was led away to a taxi cab.

Sylvie froze. Gasped in surprised shock.

She saw herself in that photo. Her eight year old self, and the crushed, defeated parents who were never the same again after that day.

"A gift to you," Jeremy said into her ear, and she whipped her head around to look at him.

"Manahan's records went *all the way* back. Turns out he got his start in the firm that foreclosed on your parents' house. He was the one that made it happen."

The video continued. "Copies of these records have been sent to the offices of the District Attorney and the US Attorney. No doubt they will want to give Manahan their own award. You do not need to give him yours."

Jeremy raised his glass toward her, for a toast. Deep affection, and pride at a job well done welled up within him.

Sylvie found that she was tearing up. She just looked at him, speechless for a second. Then she sniffed. Hard. And raised her own glass.

The two glasses touched, and a little bell seemed to ring, more beautiful than even touching crystal could make.

"Thank you," she said.

He smiled and lifted his glass to his lips.

She did the same.

ODIN'S PEPPERMINT

This story features one of my favorite characters: Dustin Cofield, Elfsterminator.

I have written a whole bunch of stories about Dustin's adventures defending the world and Christmas against the ever-present menace of rebellious elves. It's always super fun hanging out with Dustin and company, and I intend to spend a lot more time with him in the future.

Hopefully you'll feel the same.

Enjoy!

The elfin menace against the integrity and joy of Christmas goes on, behind the scenes and under the noses of the normies of the world.

I've been working to head off that menace, to keep Christmas alive and joyful, for over a decade now. I work out of an office in a Wells Fargo branch, pretending to be a financial analyst. But I don't work for the bank. I work for an agency that no one has ever heard of, because it doesn't exist.

But still, every now and then the normie world and my world collide. And when that happens, you never know what the result will be.

I'm Dustin Cofield, and I'm an Elfsterminator

When Crystal called me on the old rotary phone in my office, I was just finishing up my monthly report to Higher Headquarters. And frankly I was thankful for the break; my fingers and wrists were starting to ache from the effort.

Typing on an old 30s-era manual typewriter is not exactly easy, and even now after more than a decade working for the Agency and living with the lack of electronics that the Big Man required, I still wasn't completely used to it.

Or rather, I still hadn't learned not to dislike it.

So it was with near-relief that I turned away from the page, complete with carbon paper forms in triplicate, to pick up the call.

"How's it going, Cofield?" Crystal said as soon as I had the receiver to my ear. I recognized her voice immediately, even though it had been a few months since we last worked together.

"Crystal! Good to hear from you."

She cut right to the chase. "I'm in town on an op, and I could use some help. Are you free?"

I looked at the report, and did some typing math in my head. It would take a couple hours to finish, proofread it, and get it packaged for the dispatches. But after that I didn't have anything major on my plate until the middle of next week.

It had been a quiet month in Lockwood, the pleasantly nice but cookie-cutter suburban city I had been stationed in these last few years. Not even a hint of illicit elfin activity, and as autumn rolled on toward Thanksgiving I had begun to think— hope, really—that I might get a free holiday season to just enjoy for the first time in...

I struggled to think of the last time that had happened, to be honest. And got a little depressed for a second.

But only a second. Sure I'd missed more Christmases than I'd like since joining up. But I'd helped guarantee Christmas bliss for more people than I could count. So it was worth it.

"I can meet you in the morning. That soon enough?"

"Perfect. You know that breakfast joint over on Elm Street?"

McGillicutty's it was called. I knew it well. Nora, my girl-friend, and I made a point of going to their Sunday brunches once a month or so. They made great pastries, and did bottom-less mimosas.

Hard to beat.

I nodded, though Crystal couldn't see it. "Nine o'clock?"

She agreed, and hung up.

McGillicutty's didn't look like much from the outside. It sat in the corner of an L-shaped strip mall a quarter mile from the beltway that traversed the metropolitan areas Lockwood inhab-ited. Like most strip malls everywhere, it was a single story, bland beige-brown with eaves overhanging the shopfronts and a modest-sized parking lot that was never more or less than half-filled with cars.

But every time I crossed the threshold into McGillicutty's, I was always struck by its simple class; it's charm.

It was set up like a modernized diner almost, with a long bar taking up most of the right-hand side wall and reddish-brown leather upholstered booths for six along the wall opposite the bar. The space between was filled with tables for four, also with leather-upholstered chairs of the same color. The bar stools were the same.

The bar itself was topped by black granite, flaked with bits of gold and brown, and the area behind the bar was all stainless steel appliances and black shelves, holding more plates and cups than bottles of liquor...though it was not lacking in those. And the section of the bar facing the entrance, catty-corner to the sitting area, was dominated by a glass display case that filled with donuts, pies, danishes, coffee cakes...everything a sweet tooth could want first thing in the morning.

The place always smelled of freshly-baked bread and sweets overtop coffee, and smooth jazz played softly from speakers hidden in the corners of the room.

It was instant welcoming relaxation every time.

When I arrived that morning I did a quick scan of the room, ignoring the perky young brunette in a blue polo shirt with McGillicutty's embroidered in white on the left breast who was holding court at the hostess' station, a darkly-stained wooden lectern just in front of the door.

The place was about a third full. The usual late-breakfast crowd of moms who had just dropped kids off at school and were now gathering over coffee to gossip or do whatever groups of moms did, business types in suits who were wolfing down Danishes over coffee while reading the paper, and artsy folks typing away on laptops while their frothy something-chino drinks cooled next to them.

And Crystal, alone in the rear-most booth.

She had her blonde hair pulled back from her head into a pony tail, and she was dressed in a navy-blue business skirt and collared white shirt. A fair match to the charcoal-grey banker's suit with blue and white tie that I had on.

She had the lean body of a dancer, because she was. She used to be in a semi-professional ballet troupe, but the incident of 2013 hit her hard, and she joined the Agency soon after, looking for payback.

From what I knew of her exploits, and from the cases we'd worked together, she had gotten it. In spades.

The hostess greeted me, and I smiled back at her and gestured toward Crystal, saying, "My party is here."

She nodded and I meandered on back to Crystal's booth.

Crystal saw me coming, of course, and the corners of her mouth twitched upward. Her eyes flicked up and down, taking in my suit, and I thought I saw a bit of amusement there for a second.

"Been a while," she said as I slid into the booth opposite her. "How's Nora?"

I smiled. "Busy. The work she did for the new Ford plant gave her a lot of exposure, and she's had to beat clients away with a stick the last few months."

"I heard about your little adventure there." Crystal shook her head. "Bold of the pointies, trying that."

My smile faded. The elves had tried to set up their own hidden production facility inside the Ford plant. To supplant the Big Guy's up at the Pole, no doubt. And they would have succeeded if Nora's project management skills hadn't led her to discover a discrepancy that I followed up on.

A midnight raid put the kibosh on the pointies' plans, but I cringed to think of what mischief they could have gotten up to if we hadn't stopped their plant within a plant from coming online.

After a second, I shrugged. "All in a day's work. What do you have going on?"

"An interesting little mystery," she began, but paused when a young black-haired man in the same kind of polo shirt the hostess was wearing approached our table. He was carrying a brown plastic tray on which sat two plates with cinnamon buns and a teapot with two mugs.

"Here we go," the waiter said and proceeded to set a plate before each of us. Then he took a moment to pour a mug of black tea for us both and set the teapot down between us.

Then he departed, leaving me to raise an eyebrow at Crystal.

She grinned slyly at me. "I hear the cinnamon buns here are to die for."

I nodded slowly. She was correct, of course. I'd never had better than the buns McGillicutty's made. Still... "Maybe I want some bacon and eggs."

Crystal rolled her eyes. "Then order it. Seriously, Cofield." Her tone said I was being silly, and as she raised her bun to her mouth to take a bite I decided her tone was right.

The bun went down real well. It was still warm from the oven, and the icing had an almost peppermint undertone to it.

Nora had several times asked me, jokingly, if the owners maybe also secretly moonlighted for the Big Guy, on account of that.

I should be so lucky. I'd been up to the Pole a few years ago for an awards gala, and to call the cuisine up there disappointing...

"The pointies have been branching out financially," Crystal said, interrupting my train of thought.

I stopped mid-chew and raised an eyebrow at her. Since they left the Pole in protest over working conditions, they'd been making their way in the world mostly the way anyone else would have. Starting businesses, getting jobs, what have you. It wasn't like there was some grand elfin infrastructure or anything.

But their ventures tended to ride the fuzzy line between legitimate and criminal, and they usually had each others' backs. And they all wanted payback against the Big Guy.

So it wasn't unusual to find that the elves had wormed their way into a new business of some sort or other. And really I didn't begrudge them that; nor did the Agency. Except when it impacted the Big Guy's operation or had the potential to.

I swallowed the bit of bun I had been chewing and washed it down with a sip of tea. "How so?"

"I've been working on a sort of retail arbitrage operation a group of them have going out west. Teddy Bears, matchbox cars..." She made a vague wave of her hand. "It'll take too long to get into. Point is, lots of cash changing hands. But also electronic transactions. Mostly what you'd expect from the sorts of things they were trading in. But there were a few transfers that don't make any sense."

"How do you mean?"

Crystal shrugged. "Mostly in where the money is going to. Bank accounts that don't appear to intersect with the pointies at all. Not tied to any businesses they have a hand in, just to normies or legit businesses."

"Well not everything the pointies do is dirty," I pointed out. "Could just be legit purchases."

"Could be." She leaned in a bit. "Or maybe not. I need some help running the accounts down, figuring out what's going on."

"Why me?"

"You've got a degree in finance don't you? That's why you have that cover?"

"Yeah, but it's been ages since I did anything with it. Just cause my office is in a bank doesn't mean—" I stopped, the hairs on the back of my neck standing up as I felt a realization dawning, and just looked the next question at her.

Crystal nodded, her expression grimly serious. "Nailed it in one. The accounts are all at Wells Fargo."

I blew out a breath and considered, then shook my head. "I just have an office there as cover. I don't have access to their system, to go digging in their records, if that's what you're thinking."

"Ask the branch manager to look at subparagraph 6, section F of the contract they signed with the Agency."

I blinked. I knew the bank was making a pretty decent penny from the "rent" on my office space, and for the branch manager to maintain the facade that I actually was a senior financial analyst for the bank. But I'd never seen the contract that set the whole thing in place.

My confusion must have shown on my face because Crystal grinned broadly. "It allows you executive-level access."

I blinked again. It did?

"Same thing at my cover location. I didn't know about it either until about a year ago. Turns out it's a standard clause in the Agency's contracts." She reached down to her right, where she must have left a briefcase on the booth seat next to her. A moment later she came back up with a manila envelope which she slid across the table to me. "The accounts and transfers in question."

I fingered the envelope for a second, then shrugged. "Ok, I'll have a look into it."

"Whatever you can find out," she said. "Thanks in advance."

It looked like my anticipated lazy end to the week was about to turn interesting.

Tom Jenkins was the branch manager at the Wells Fargo where I had my office. We'd known each other for several years now and got along pretty well for the most part. It helped that we only saw each other once or twice a week for staff meetings that I had to attend to keep up appearances, and that I never owed him any actual work product.

And that the Agency's payments made his branch a perennial stand-out in quarterly profits.

But today the normally jovial grin was gone from his round face. His grey eyes flashed with annoyance beneath the gleam of the overhead lights reflecting off the dome of his bald head.

We were in his office, in the rear corner of the bank. It was all faux hardwood and modern-looking brushed nickel. Sterile and efficient, even to his metal-legged glass-topped desk, which was devoid of the clutter you would except on a working surface.

Just a flat-screen monitor to the left, a keyboard on a calendar blotter in the center, and a single framed picture of his wife—a raven-haired woman about ten years younger than Tom's forty-five—off to the right.

Like me he wore a banker's suit. But his was navy blue and pinstriped, his tie deep red.

Tom scowled at me for a second, then looked back at his monitor screen and re-read the contract with the Agency.

It was his third time reading that paragraph. Each time he just got madder.

Finally, scowling even deeper, he leaned back in his chair and stared a dagger at me. "It seems you have me over a barrel."

"I wouldn't call it that, Tom."

"Well how would you call it then?"

I spread my hands and smiled magnanimously at him. "The paragraph is just a guarantee of mutual cooperation. Nothing more."

He snorted, rolling his eyes to the ceiling. "Semantics." Then after a couple seconds he blew out a breath and looked back at me, his face smoothed back to professional calm. It was great how he could do that so quickly. "What do you need, Mr. Cofield?"

I placed the manila folders Crystal had given me down on his desk next to his keyboard. "It's all in there. I need a deep dive on those accounts and transactions. See if anything stands out, waves a red flag."

Tom's eyebrow twitched and he looked at the envelope like it might be dangerous.

And he had to think that it just might be. After all, the Agency couldn't go around calling itself "the outfit that makes sure the Big Guy's Pole operation goes well so Christmas goes off without a hitch each year."

No, we had cover here in the States as a branch of DHS, and he had to be wondering what I was getting his branch involved in.

But after a minute, he nodded. "I'll put Alice on it. When do you need an answer?"

It was Thursday morning. Tomorrow, Monday, and Tuesday were the only working days before my schedule got tight again.

"Tomorrow afternoon, close of business."

Tom looked like he was going to object, but he just nodded again. "Consider it done."

It was Monday morning. Alice had been able to glean a veritable treasure trove of information, and I'd spent the weekend using the Agency's considerable resources to do a deeper analysis on what she had given me.

Now, Crystal and I sat in my souped-up black GMC Yukon across the street from a long, low building that was painted yellow and had a red-brown tile roof. A simple chain link fence surrounded the building's property and I could see a swing set and a jungle gym off to the right, around the building's corner. A small parking lot was off to the left, with room for maybe a dozen cars.

A wood sign, red letters on a yellow background, hung over the building's front door. KinderKids Pre-School and Daycare.

Crystal was sipping on a Starbucks cup in the passenger seat. We'd met there and I'd driven us both here after she had a chance to caffeine-up.

Today she had on black trousers and a button-collared red blouse that hung loosely around her torso. She had the top two buttons undone, and her hair was down, flowing to her shoulders in lush curls.

"What are we doing here, Cofield?" she asked.

"Waiting for our man."

She looked sidelong at me, and her lips compressed slightly into a half-scowl that was offset by the amused twinkle in her eyes. "And our man is...?"

"The owner of this fine establishment." I gestured toward the daycare facility. "Most of the transactions you gave me were blanks, but half a dozen of them went to accounts that were owned by this business, either directly or through intermediaries that I was able to run down. Something is going down here."

Crystal blinked. "Ok, so who is he?"

"Guy named Olaf Gunterman."

She peered around, looking both ways down the four-lane street that ran in front of the daycare. "What's he look like?"

"He stands out. You'll see when he gets here."

Crystal glowered again, and I grinned back at her. "Don't want to spoil the surprise."

Instead of replying, she took another drink from her cup. A much longer drink.

About ten minutes passed, and I could tell Crystal was beginning to get impatient. But then a dark blue BMW pulled up in front of the daycare and turned into the parking lot. I recognized the car from the DMV records I'd been able to pull and gave Crystal a little nudge.

"There he is."

We each had binoculars, and she raised hers to get a better look at Gunterman. A second later she gave a little gasp and said, "Oh my," in a low, almost sultry tone.

Gunterman was six foot three. Blond, with wavy hair that flowed past his linebacker-sized shoulders like Fabio reimagined. He had on khaki cargo pants and a green, collared shirt beneath a black leather jacket, and he was jacked.

The kind of jacked that only comes from working out three or four hours a day, five or six days a week, for twenty years. That kind of jacked.

"Yeah, we're definitely going to need to look into *him* more closely," Crystal said.

I couldn't help it; I burst out laughing.

Over the next hour a steady stream of parents in sedans and minivans came to the daycare and dropped off their kids, and the swings and jungle gym began to fill up with kids doing kid things and having a good time.

I wasn't exactly a daycare aficionado; no kids for me, that I knew of anyway. But it looked as normal a scene as I could have imagined.

Except for those financial records, and the other facts I'd gleaned from them over the weekend.

"I dunno, Cofield," Crystal said, lowering her binoculars and looking back at me with a doubtful expression on her face. "You sure about this?"

I nodded. "There's *something* going on over there, no doubt about it."

She chewed on her lip for a second, then gave a firm nod. "Ok." She opened the passenger door of the Yukon. "Come on."

"What are we—?"

"I'm expecting. And you, hubby, are coming with me to look at daycare options for our soon-to-arrive bundle of joy." She grinned and patted her—flat as a board—belly.

Well, she could pass for just a couple months along, I supposed. And I didn't have a better idea, so I hopped out as well and we crossed the street through a gap in traffic.

The front door opened into a reception area that reminded me immediately of a doctor's office. There were half a dozen plastic blue chairs on the wall to the right of the entrance and an end table in the corner on which was stacked a like number of magazines. A sliding clear plastic window directly across from the entrance looked in on the reception desk, and a door leading further back into the innards of the building was to the left.

The reception desk was manned by a redhead with pixie-cut hair who looked to be in her early 30s. She had on a green long-sleeved collar shirt with KinderKids embroidered on the breast, and she was typing away at a computer keyboard when Crystal and I walked in.

Crystal went straight to the window and slid it open, and the receptionist gave a little start of surprise that turned into a broad, welcoming grin that made her look five years younger.

"Good morning! Welcome to KinderKids," she said in a lilting accent that made me think she actually was Irish to go with her hair.

Crystal began giving our cover story. It only took a moment for the receptionist to get the gist of it—it probably was a regular occurrence here—and she called back on an intercom to someone farther back in the building.

A minute or so later the door to the left opened and another woman, this one approaching forty with curly black hair and eyes that were nearly the same shade stepped through. She had on a similar shirt to the receptionist's and blue jeans, and a welcoming smile.

"I'm Sheila," she said and held out her hand in greeting. "I understand you want some more information about our facilities?"

Crystal shook and gave her real first name. I did the same. A moment later we were following Sheila down a white-painted hallway.

"We've been in business for eight years," Sheila was saying, "and have served over two thousand families. We utilize the latest--"

I let Crystal keep up the conversation, play the eager expecting mother. I put Sheila's discourse out of my mind and focused on the facilities.

Which were nothing if not ordinary. Well kept. Neat and tidy, painted in cheerful tones with pictures of playing kids and beautiful scenery up on the walls. Classrooms and play rooms with bookshelves and all the toys I ever could have wanted when I was a munchkin. A segregated office area through a door that I only got a glimpse through as one of the staffers was passing.

And everywhere, kids. Lots and lots of kids, all looking like they were having a good time, for a wonder.

Kids voices talking and giggling and laughing—and occasionally crying—filled the spaces of the building as we walked through. And I began to wonder if Crystal wasn't correct and we were barking up the wrong tree.

But the transaction analysis was clear. There were just enough questionable things there. Just enough middle men and obvious reporting loopholes used to make me certain things weren't completely legit here.

But then maybe it was just regular run of the mill criminality, not pointy-related. Gunterman may not have known who or what those transfers came from, after all.

I was just about to call this a waste of time when Sheila brought us to a door with a narrow glass window in it. She gestured toward the window and said, "This is our arts and crafts room," with obvious pride.

Peering through the narrow window I could see why. The place was large, well-lit, and well equipped with easels and craft tables, every color of paint and every little construction tool imaginable. Building blocks and you name it, all stored neatly in white plastic shelves in the wall to the left.

The room was also filled with kids under the supervision of a trio of adults. Nothing at all unusual there.

Except for the long table at the rear of the room and the trio of plastic jugs behind it. The jugs looked to be at least five to ten gallons each, and translucent, filled with a greenish fluid. A couple of kids were working at the table in front of the jugs, older than most of the others in the room.

And they moved with more coordination than the others.

The hackles of my neck went up again as I watched those

kids in the rear of the room, and I saw one of them, a black-haired girl in a yellow and red striped shirt, brush her hair back from her face.

And I saw the pointed tip of an ear exposed for a heartbeat.

I glanced aside at Crystal and saw her eyes widen; she had seen it too.

Our eyes met, and she gave a little nod.

We were definitely in the right spot, after all.

"I want a look at those jugs in the back of that room," I said as we drove away.

Crystal nodded. "Come back tonight?"

"Yep," I said. And inwardly, I sighed.

That meant the combat suit. I hated the combat suit.

When I first saw the combat suit that the Agency issues to its personnel, I thought it was a joke on the new guy. Alas, it wasn't.

The suit is made from the same material that the Big Guy's wife uses to make his clothing, and something about the centuries that the Big Guy and the elves spent together created a resonance or a recognition or a something embedded into that material, so it repels a lot of the elves' tricks.

So it looks ridiculous: made from red fuzzy material with a broad fuzzy white belt with equipment pouches and a sidearm holster, and with a pull-up red and white hood and half-face mask. And fuzzy white gloves. It looks like a demented mix of Santa Suit and burglar attire.

But it's effective and protective. It had saved my butt several times over the years.

So though I feel like an absolutely idiot every time I have to put the thing on, and it can get really hot especially in the summer, I still use it.

Just wish we could try a different color scheme at least. But that suggestion had been shot down faster than a nerd in the cheerleader's locker room. Powers that be in HQ didn't want to take any chances at breaking the magic or whatever it was that made the material work. So we used the Big Guy's colors and that's it.

Oh well.

Crystal and I met up a bit before midnight a couple blocks from KinderKids, in the rear parking lot of a mattress store. It was dark, and the wooded area at the rear of the lot ran all the way down to the cross street that held the daycare spot. So we could creep up without getting anywhere near any street lights.

I'd looked at aerial shots of the daycare's lot on Google Maps, so it was pretty easy to navigate there from the lot. Maybe twenty minutes after we met up, we stopped at the fence at the rear of the daycare and took stock.

The fence was chain link back here, and seven feet tall. Easy enough to scale, but...

Crystal had lowlight goggles pressed to her eyes and was scanning the building.

"Anything?" I asked.

She shook her head. "No cameras that I can see."

I frowned. That was surprising. "I would think they'd want to have eyes on the kids all the time, for liability if nothing else."

She shrugged. "The playground's off to the side. Maybe the cameras are there."

Which was a valid point. The rear of the building, where

we were, was just grass and a couple storage sheds, and a paved walk going from the sheds to the rear door of the building, and then to the right-hand side of the building and probably up to the parking lot. Another section of fence separated the play area to the left from this rear space, so maybe the kids never came back here.

And surely management wouldn't want records of whatever the pointies were doing. So the no cameras here, where they could come and go in plain sight, almost?

I nodded. "Ok. Up and over."

Chain link fences aren't hard to scale, but they are annoying. It took longer than it should have for me to get over, and Crystal stood waiting, arms crossed over her chest with an amused half-smirk on her lips when I finally managed it.

I returned her smirk with a shrug. Easy for her to criticize, all hundred ten pounds of ballerina muscle that she was.

The thought must have carried through in volumes with my shrug, because she chuckled softly, then led the way to the back door.

The Agency teaches its operatives how to deal with locks, and the one on the back door wasn't particularly difficult. A few minutes later we were inside. We each took a moment to don lowlight goggles, then we made our way to the arts and crafts room.

The door was locked. Naturally. And this lock was more difficult, but I managed to get it open after what felt like forever.

The jugs at the back of the room were less full than they had been when we toured the facilities. In fact only one of them had any fluid in it at all, the right-most one. I glanced at Crystal and frowned.

"Either they used a lot of paint, or..." She left the rest unsaid.

I snorted. These jugs weren't paint. The paint was stored elsewhere in the room; we'd seen that earlier.

I moved to the right-most jug, and saw that it had a screwed-on lid at the top. I came off easily, and I had to move back from the intense smell of peppermint that immediately wafted from the thing.

"Good Lord," I said, scrunching up my nose against the onslaught.

"That is...strong," Crystal said. She was about ten feet away and hadn't taken as much of a hit as I had, but I could hear the near-affront in her voice from the smell of it.

"Yeah, what is—"

My lowlight goggles whited out completely, and I heard an accented voice from behind us.

"Put your hands up."

I froze and immediately realized what had happened. Someone had turned on the lights.

We were caught in the act of burglary.

It wouldn't be a huge problem; the Agency would grease the skids with local cops to get us released and no harm done. But that would be annoying and waste time.

And we'd never hear the end of it from the other operatives.

But right then there didn't seem to be a lot I could do about that so I did what the voice said and raised my hands, taking a second to doff the lowlight goggles as I did so.

"Turn around," the voice said.

I complied and was unsurprised to see Olaf Gunterman standing in the arts and crafts room, just inside the door.

I *was* surprised by the AR he had shouldered and pointing at us.

The combat suit looked ridiculous, but it was good protection against elfin weapons and tricks. No good at all against a 5.56mm rifle round, though.

Gunterman looked at us for a few seconds, then shook his head and chuckled softly. "You know, the little guys told me about you people. I thought they were kidding."

I blinked. That was...unexpected.

"What do you do, Gunterman, sleep here?"

Gunterman shook his head again. "Silent alarm to my phone." He grinned. "Technology is pretty cool. Might wanna try it." He paused, then put on a mocking expression. "Oh. Wait. You can't, on account of the Big Guy." He shrugged. "Tough luck for you."

That came like a slap to the face. I looked aside at Crystal and saw she was as stunned as I was, by his knowledge.

"So you clearly know who—what—you're working with in this," I said, slowly and levelly, trying to keep the surprise out of my voice and—I think—mostly succeeding.

Gunterman grinned. "Santa's former little helpers? Oh yeah, we know each other well." He wagged his rifle at us. "Come this way. Slowly."

I did as he said, happy to close the distance. If he let us get close enough, maybe we could do something to get past that rifle.

I wasn't sure what. But I knew I couldn't do a damn thing from the other side of the room. So I walked slowly.

Crystal moved in time with me. "But if you know..." Crystal sounded genuinely curious, "then why?"

"Why help them?" Gunterman's grin faded. "I've prayed to Odin for years for a way to get back on the people who destroyed my nation."

That went right over my head. "Come again?"

Gunterman looked at me like I was daft. Couldn't blame him; right then I felt like I was. "Before the Christians came, my people were the scourge of the North, feared by all. We sailed everywhere, conquered everywhere, plundered everywhere, favored by the gods." He scowled, an angry light in his eyes. "Now what are we? Weak. Willingly cuckolded in every way. A mockery of what we once were." He drew in a rasping breath. "If Christmas is so important to the Christian, I say ruin it, as they ruined my people."

It took me a few seconds to really process that.

I'd met people who didn't like Christmas. But not that many. Most people I'd met enjoyed it, whether they were Christians or not. Heck my Orthodox Jewish friend used to come caroling with me back in the day, just because he liked the music, the ambiance, and the companionship of it.

But even the people I met who didn't like Christmas were never this actively hostile.

This guy was something else.

We had crossed half of the distance between the jugs and him, and he waved the rifle again. "That's far enough."

I stopped, and Crystal did as well. "So what happens now?"

Gunterman looked us over for a second. "That is the question. I could call the cops and you can go down for burglary." His paralleling of my earlier thoughts felt eerie. "But I expect you'll get out of that easy enough."

Yeah, really eerie.

Gunterman went on. "My little friends might have some fun with you. Maybe I'll give you to them."

That was actually a more scary concept than the cops. The cops were constrained by rules and laws. The pointies were not, except as expedience required. It didn't happen often, but there had been a few operatives over the years who had been taken captive by the elves.

It had not turned out well for those guys. Years of recovery and therapy later, and they still had uncontrollable sugar rushes from out of nowhere—irresistible urges to drink cocoa nonstop or snort sugar.

I shuddered inwardly to think of it.

"But then again," Gunterman said, "this is a war. Why take prisoners in a war?"

He shifted his stance ever so slightly, leaning into his weapon a bit more than he had been, like he was getting ready to shoot.

"So you're just going to shoot us in cold blood?"

He made a quick shake of his head in response to Crystal's query. "You pulled guns on me."

Cute suggestion but the tinsel guns we carried in our holsters weren't exactly deadly weapons. But then again, after we were dead, he could just plant real guns on us couldn't he?

The state Lockwood inhabited was pretty liberal in its self-defense and weapons laws. Might not even be much of an inquiry about it if he staged it right.

"You're overlooking one thing," Crystal said.

"Oh?" Gunterman didn't do the contemptuous conde-scending tone like victorious bad guys do in movies, but he came close to it. "What's that?"

In response, Crystal squeezed her left hand and something squirted out. It was red, and it flew through the air toward Gunterman's face.

It took me a second to realize it had happened and the thing, whatever it was, was actually real.

It took Gunterman a heartbeat longer than me. I started moving left as his eyes widened in surprise. Crystal darted to the right.

A shot rang out—LOUD—and I threw myself to the ground.

Then Gunterman let out a strangled cry.

I looked up and saw that the red stuff, whatever it was, had splattered on his forehead and had coated his face from the bridge of his nose to the top of his head like wax dripping from a candle.

His eyes were completely covered; he couldn't see, and for a moment he didn't do anything except move his left hand from the hand guard of his rifle to clutch at the stuff that had suddenly blinded him.

Moving with instinct, I drew my tinsel gun from its holster, aimed, and fired.

From the right, I heard the sound of Crystal's gun going off as well.

A second later, Gunterman was wrapped head to toe in silvery-white cords that could only come off with the solvent I carried in one of my belt pouches.

His rifle clattered to the ground. His wrapped-up body followed suit a moment later, and I stood up slowly.

Looking to the right, I saw Crystal also rising and was relieved to see she had not been struck by Gunterman's shot.

I turned to look behind us and saw that the bullet had struck the rightmost jug, the one that still had fluid in it. That fluid was now dripping out of the hole the bullet had made and then down onto the floor.

It was so green it was almost black, and viscous like molasses. A little trail of steam or smoke rose from the surface it was flowing down as it moved; I got the impression the stuff was eating away at it.

I swallowed. Hard. Then looked back at Crystal.

"What was that you shot him with?"

She grinned at me. "Spiked Eggnog."

I blinked. "What the hell was it spiked with? And what did you shoot it from? Your hand was empty."

Crystal's grin expanded beyond what I'd ever seen from her. "A girl's got to keep *some* secrets, Cofield."

Crystal and I had typed up reports in my office a time or two in the past, but this time felt different. Because I didn't really know the whole story.

Oh we'd figured out what the goop in the jugs was. Colleen down at my evidence lab had run some analyses and determined it was basically peppermint spice, except it had been spiked with compounds that would build up in a person's system and destroy good cheer.

Apparently the plan had been to spike candy supplies and restaurants in town all over the metro area, and if it worked well this year, expand the operation state-wide next year, then further out from there.

If we hadn't caught it and nipped it in the bud now, in a couple years' time it might have been impossible to put that genie back in the bottle.

No, what I still didn't get was how Crystal had shot him with that egg nog. And it irked me.

She sat in one of the two simple wooden chairs in front of the massive old desk that dominated most of my office, and was finishing up reading the last page of the report.

I watched her and found I was frowning.

She noticed it when she looked up from the page. She opened her mouth to speak, then stopped, cocking her head to the side slightly. "What?"

"You gonna tell me how you did that eggnog bit?"

Crystal blinked, then burst out laughing. "Really? You haven't figured it out?"

I shook my head.

"Cofield, you're a guy. Do you have any idea how much stronger you are than a woman, even one as strong as me?"

"Yes. Yes, I do."

She shook her head. "I don't think you do, not in your gut.

Well, I know it. Every woman does. If I get into grappling range with a guy your size, I'm probably done. So I've made some modifications to my combat suit. One of those things is an eggnog bladder in my sleeve and squeeze-shooter in my gloves."

"The Agency let you do that?"

She shrugged. "What they don't know won't hurt them."

Couldn't argue with that. But...

"How much time do you practice with that thing? That was one hell of a shot."

She hesitated for a second, then let out a little shrug. "To be honest I'd never really used it before. It was one of those cool ideas that you almost forget about, know what I mean?"

"You're kidding."

"Nope. But if he was about to shoot us I figured what could it hurt to try it?" Her expression turned deadly grave. "We got real lucky."

I just nodded silently.

After a few seconds, Crystal put the final page down on the stack of report pages, in triplicate of course, that sat on the edge of my desk closest to her. Then she picked all the pages up and stood.

"Well I'd better get back on the road for home. I'll take care of filing this if it's ok with you?"

I waved a dismissive hand. "It's your case. I'm just as happy to not deal with it."

She flashed a grin at me. "Thanks for the help, Cofield. Say hi to Nora for me."

Then she turned and left the office. The door closed behind her with a solid, final thump and I leaned back in my chair.

She wasn't kidding. We really had been lucky. Very lucky.

I looked at the counterweight-powered wall clock across the room from the door. It was four thirty. Nora would be getting off work in an hour. We hadn't planned to meet up until the day after tomorrow, but right then I felt strongly the need to see her.

So I picked up the phone.

She answered on the second ring.

An hour and a half later I knocked on her door, and she let me in.

A NOSE FOR TACOS

Romance is, by far, the biggest selling fiction genre. I am not, strictly speaking, a romance writer, but sometimes I like to dip my toe in because it's fun and, let's face it, we're all a little bit romantic at heart. Even cold, calculating former Naval Officers turned writers.

This is a fun meet-cute, set on one of the beaches here in San Diego.

Enjoy!

How did people ever survive without glasses?

Logically Kyle knew that wasn't a problem for many, probably most, people throughout history. But then most people don't have the 20/300 uncorrected vision that he did.

Still, just then as he was down on his knees grabbing around for the spectacles that had just been knocked off his head, that question flashed through his mind.

And then he saw only stars as something smacked him across the side of his head, and he fell the rest of the way to the ground.

Laughter from above, and the flare of pain from his nose as it impacted with the gravelly pavement of the blacktop he had been standing on just a few moments ago drove all thought from his mind for a moment that felt like an eternity.

He lay there, breathing through his mouth and tasting the stone below him.

And groaned.

The laughter stopped and a rhythmic thumping sounded on the pavement next to him, then from the corner of his eye a blurry shape came to a halt at his side.

"Kyle, you alright, dude?"

Kyle pushed himself back up onto his hand and knees, ignoring the throbbing in his nose, and then rolled over into a sitting position and looked up at the shape.

This close he could recognize Tim, mostly. Straight but still tousled light brown hair that hung to just above his shoulders. Deep brown eyes in a narrow face that was pinched in concern. He wore loose-fitting dark blue athletic shorts and a white tank top made of wicking material; his chest muscles were clearly visible, what little of them he had.

He kept on dribbling his basketball as he awaited Kyle's response.

Kyle reached up to touch his nose and hissed as a new lance of pain struck him. "Mighta broke my nose," he said.

Tim winced, and ceased dribbling the basketball, holding up his right hand, palm open, toward the hoop that Kyle and his friends had been playing at.

From over toward the hoop, Kyle heard Jack and Jose shuffle to a stop, and Jose said, "Sorry man. Tried to pass to you, and..." He left off the rest; what else needed saying?

It became clear what had happened. The ball had taken an errant bounce, or Jose hadn't noticed Kyle lose his glasses, and his head was in the wrong place at the wrong time.

An accident. Still sucked.

Kyle shrugged and pushed himself to his feet. His knees and the palms of his hands felt sore and scraped, a shallow pool next to the ocean of hurt that was his nose, and he felt his left knee pop slightly as he reached his feet.

"Any of you guys see my glasses?"

The blurry shapes that Kyle could just barely recognize as Jose and Jack swiveled around. Jack had on a red shirt and black shorts, Jose green and grey. After a second Jack said, "Yeah," and bounded over to a place a few feet over to Kyle's left.

Jack held out his hand and a few seconds later Kyle had his glasses on, to the protest of his nose, and the world came back into existence.

It was a sunny day; but then it was almost always sunny in San Diego. White puffy clouds dotted the sky at mid-altitude, moving slowly to the east from the prevailing winds. A bit after noon, the March day was well into the mid-70s. Especially by the sea in Ocean Beach, where they were playing, it almost never got much warmer than that, even in the depths of summer.

The court they were playing on was one of three set up in a recreational area just off the beach. Behind their hoop past a bathroom building the seaside road carried a steady stream of cars past a two-story blocky apartment complex directly ahead and then a long line of single story beach bungalow-style houses that cost more than Kyle even wanted to consider in today's market.

Opposite their hoop, the grey-white sand ran down to the beach where the surf was breaking, lending the faint scent of brine to the gentle offshore breeze, and girls were sunning themselves. A few wetsuit-clad surfers were braving the waves, small as they were, and further north a half mile or so people were running their dogs along the surf at the Dog Beach.

The other two courts were taken by larger groups who were playing full-court. Kyle and his buddies were just doing half-court, but even still he had been working up a sweat; his shirt, a blue and white keepsake from last year's San Diego Half Marathon, was plastered to his chest.

"You good to go, bro?" Jose asked.

He was a head taller than Kyle and all lean muscle; the only one of their group who could actually dunk. He kept his black hair trimmed short, almost in a high and tight, and he had gold hoop earrings in both ears. A black tattoo of a crucifix adorned his left forearm and he sported a tiny tuft of hair at the end of his chin.

Jose was looking at Kyle with a mixture of concern and eagerness to continue.

Kyle reached up to touch his nose again and winced. Then winced a bit more when his fingers came away red; his nose was bleeding.

"I'm going to sit down for a minute," he said, and Jose nodded.

"There's some ice in the cooler," Jack said.

They had placed their cooler and bags down on the side of the court adjoining the parking lot for the beach. Kyle gave a little wave to his friends, then turned toward it. Behind him, he heard the ball begin to bounce again, then the shwoosh of chains as one of the other guys, probably Jack, dropped it in.

Nothing but net.

"Ouch, that's gotta hurt!"

Sarah was reading a paperback—the latest Cussler—in her folding beach chair. The sunlight bathed her in pleasant warmth, giving her a sense of calm that balanced the frenetic pace of the book's action, leaving her in a state of pure enjoyment.

She and her friends had picked a spot back from the surf, near the basketball courts. Sarah had insisted; she had no desire to go into the bone-cold water that graced San Diego's shores. And a couple times in the past, people running past closer to the surf had kicked sand into her stuff.

She liked the beach, but hated sand. So she never went near the surf anymore. Back a ways where she could still get a good view of things but also not suffer such calamities again suited her just fine.

Carol and Deena thought her silly. But they didn't fight her on it.

Much.

It helped that there were often a bunch of cute guys playing on the courts, Sarah supposed.

She hadn't been paying attention today, though. Her book was nearing its climax and she was fully sunk down into it.

Deena's comment pulled her out of it, though. The ER nurse in her forcing her to pay attention.

"What?"

She looked to the right toward Deena, raising a questioning eyebrow.

Deena was the looker of their trio of friends. Taller than either Sarah or Carol, with naturally-bronzed skin, flowing black hair, and boobs that strained the straps of the black bikini top she was wearing.

The guys always seemed to get sucked into her chest, but Sarah was actually thankful she didn't have to deal with being so busty. The back strain alone would probably be tiresome.

Deena had her golden-framed reflective sunglasses on, but she had them pushed up onto her forehead and she was looking off to the left, toward the courts. She pointed toward the closest one. "That guy just took a basketball to the face."

Wincing, Sarah turned to follow Deena's extended finger, and immediately saw what she was talking about.

The guy was on the short side. Maybe 5'8". Not something Sarah had an issue with, since she was all of 5'1". But she knew for a fact Deena would never look at him twice. Six feet or nothing was her standard.

And he was fairly nice-looking too. Short sandy hair, good shoulders and he didn't have a beer gut. It looked like that shirt he was wearing was from a running event, so that was a plus.

But those speculative thoughts vanished when she zeroed in on his nose. It was bleeding, quite a lot, and looked like it was cocked to the side. Probably broken from what she could see from about thirty feet away.

She didn't realize she was on her feet until she had taken a step toward him and Carol said, "Where are you going?"

Sarah looked at her, blond and pale-skinned in a red and white-striped bikini, and for a second didn't know the answer. Then she realized she was holding the first-aid kit that she always packed into her beach bag—must have grabbed it by instinct—and she held it up for her friend to see.

"Professional obligations," she said, and Carol gave a little chuckle.

She was obviously rolling her eyes behind her sunglasses.

The cooler was stocked with beer cans—mostly Mike Hess Steel Beach but with a few lesser brews thrown in to appease Jose's poor taste in beer—and ice cubes. The ice had begun to melt, making it easy to grab a couple cubes out.

Pressing them to Kyle's nose brought an immediate relief to the throbbing pain that shot from it, but not enough to make him feel enthusiastic about his prospects of not having to go to the ER.

Great way to ruin a Sunday afternoon, and he really didn't want to have to deal with hours of waiting just to get told to put some tape on his nose and take some ibuprofen for the next week.

That's what an ER trip for something like this always seemed to amount to, so what was the point in even going?

To rule out something even worse, said that little voice in the back of his head.

And so Chief doesn't yell at you about it tomorrow said a louder one.

He was just about to tell his friends that he was going when a low-pitched female voice from off to the right said, "Do you need some help?"

He turned, and found himself unable to speak for a second.

If there could be said to be a girl who exactly fit "his type" it would be this girl. She was what guys lovingly call a "spinner." Short, slender, but just curvy enough in all the right spots. Spots that the soft pink string bikini she was wearing showed off nicely.

Her hair was dark brown, and pulled back in a ponytail. She had on round-framed black sunglasses and her red-brown lips were turned up ever so slightly in a mixture of friendliness and concern.

In her left hand was a zipped-up red bag with a first-aid kit's red cross on a white field emblazoned on its side, which she held up for him to see clearly.

He realized he was staring, and shrugged to hide it. "You noticed, huh? I'm thinking about going to the ER."

She shook her head. "For something like that they'll just set your nose, tape it up, and tell you to take ibuprofen for a week." She closed the lid of his cooler and gestured toward it. "Here. Sit down. Let me have a look at it."

The way she repeated his thoughts verbatim took him aback for a second, then he chuckled and did as she said.

"Are you a doctor?"

She squatted down and unzipped her first aid bag. At his words she shook her head.

"ER nurse."

"Even better," he said, earning a grin from her in reply.

"Take your glasses off," she said as she pulled out some tape, cotton balls, and a couple sealed alcohol wipes from her bag.

He complied, and the world became blurry again.

Those glasses really didn't do him justice. They weren't bad, per se. But he was much better looking without them.

Or he would be if the bottom half of his face wasn't covered in blood from his nose.

But Sarah liked to think she was better than to look merely at the externals, so she noticed the way the sunlight glinted off his green-blue eyes and decided that yes, he was much better looking without the glasses.

But that nose was definitely broken.

She set the cotton balls, wipes, and tape down next to him atop the cooler and reached out toward his face. "This is probably going to hurt a little."

"I'm not made of porcelain," he replied, and she chuckled.

He did flinch when she touched his nose, but not much. A quick probing found the break, and she decided just to go for it.

She grabbed, pulled, and twisted—

"OW!" he said, and recoiled.

For a second it looked like he was going to fall backwards off the cooler and onto the pavement, and she grabbed his shoulders to stop him.

His momentum stopped and for a second she was looking into his eyes from just over a foot away.

She swallowed and looked away, releasing his shoulder. "Come on. It didn't hurt that much, you big baby," she said.

She tore open one of the wipes and proceeded to clean up the blood from his mouth and chin.

"How did you not see the ball coming?"

"Glasses fell off. I bent over to get them, and..." The guy shrugged. "I need to get another lanyard for them. My last one broke and I've been putting off getting a new one."

Sarah shook her head and made a sympathetic face. "Guess you won't be putting it off any longer, huh?"

"Nope."

The blood was mostly gone now. She took one of the cotton balls and tore it in half, then put half in each of his nostrils. Then she applied tape in two places on the bridge of his nose.

Sarah straightened and took a half-step back, then folded her arms over her chest and surveyed her work. Not too bad. He'd be black and blue by morning, but should be just fine.

"You can put your glasses back on now."

He did so, and grinned at her. "Nice to see you again." He reached up and felt at his nose, and the tape. "That's it?"

"As long as you don't put your face in front of any more basketballs for a couple weeks."

He laughed, and she had the impression of honest good nature and humor from it, and him.

"I'll do my best." He stood, touched his nose again, and winced. "Well thanks. I'm Kyle, by the way."

"Sarah." She took his extended hand and gave it a shake.

***

She had a good grip. Pretty, and good with her hands. Good combination.

"Thanks, Sarah. Want a beer? Least I can do." He gestured toward the cooler, and she nodded.

He retrieved two of the Steel Beach cans, handed one to her, then opened his own and took a long drink.

It was a blond ale, smooth and crisp. In the afternoon's warmth and after the throbbing in his nose, its coolness as he swallowed felt like relaxation itself flowing into him.

She sipped at hers but nodded approval. "Well, take care of that nose," she said, and turned to go.

He admired the view of her from behind as she stepped away back toward her friends. A part of him said to just let it go, get back to his game.

But man, she was cute.

"Hey," he said, and she paused, looking back at him with a questioning expression.

"You want to go over to OB Beach Club, get some fish tacos?"

Why had he said that? He hated fish tacos.

But the Beach Club was well known for their great tacos. And they had some non-fish ones too, so what the hell.

* * *

Surprise flashed through Sarah, but she shouldn't have been. In that second when they had locked eyes she could see the interest within those cute orbs of his.

Part of her said no, she didn't want anything to do with some random guy she'd just met. She just wanted to get back to Cussler and her friends.

But the earnest expression on Kyle's face, and the goofy way he looked just then with the tape and cotton balls in his nose—that she had just put there. And the way he did fill out that half marathon shirt fairly nicely...

She hadn't gone on a date in a while, not since breaking up with Jaime two months ago. She told herself she hadn't felt the lack, but right that second looking at Kyle, she realized that was a lie.

So what the hell.

"Sure," she said.

He grinned broadly, and she went to retrieve her beach bag. Then she walked beside him to get some tacos.

And maybe something more.

COSMIC PIZZA

I was having a hard time deciding what to write about, so I asked my kids for a suggestion. My youngest said, "Pizza!" And my oldest, who loves horror stories, said, "Eldritch horror!"

Lovecraftian horror and pizza, together?

CHALLENGE ACCEPTED!

Enjoy!

It was a short order pizza parlor. Million others like it, scattered throughout cities all over the country; hell, all over the world as far as Jeff knew.

There were half a dozen booths on the left wall as he walked in, large enough to seat four—six if you were friendly—and upholstered with red naugahyde. To the right, a quartet of red-tableclothed tables with straight-backed chairs for six around each. Directly ahead a darkly-stained countertop with a cash register on the left and a fountain drink dispenser with eight nozzles to the right.

The counter ended just past the register, allowing narrow egress to the rear where a brick oven stove dominated the rear wall of the cooking space. Cooling racks and white countertops provided work space for the staff, and it looked like there was a little alcove way back and to the left for a pair of restrooms.

The place smelled of baking bread, mozzarella, and tomato sauce, and felt warmly welcoming.

Except for the dead body at the last table to the right.

The man was seated with his back to the wall. He looked to be in his mid-30s. In good shape, like he went to the gym regularly. He had on blue jeans and a blue and white plaid flannel shirt, unbuttoned at the collar. His black hair was cut short on the sides and back but longer on top, flopping over the right side of his head jauntily.

He would have been a good-looking guy, except for the butcher knife sticking out of the center of his chest.

He was slumped back in his chair, his head lolled back so it contacted the wall. His eyes were wide in final shock and his mouth hung slackly open. Half-chewed pizza-slice could be visible within.

The slice he had been eating was still mostly-clenched in his right hand, now flopped onto the tabletop next to his plate. The rest of his pizza was on a raised platform in the center of his table, between his plate and that of his date, across the table from him.

Hawaiian pizza, looked like. Jeff wanted to shudder at the thought but suppressed the impulse, professional stoicism overriding the natural revulsion that abomination against nature and good taste wanted to evoke within him.

The man's date was at a different table now, closer to the door and curled up on herself as she clutched the emergency blanket a paramedic had given to her close. She was crying uncontrollably, even now a good hour or so after the incident. Her mascara had run so that her cheeks were streaks of black, and her dirty blond hair, once clearly done up nicely—or at least coherently—into a bun was now haphazard, with strings and strands popping out every which way.

A guy Jeff didn't recognize from the patrol division was sitting next to her, his notepad open and a look of exasperated patience on his face, but it was clear she wasn't saying anything worthwhile.

Two more patrol officers had another man cornered in the second booth from the rear on the left side. Though maybe maybe cornered wasn't the right word for it.

He was handcuffed, and seated in the couch's bench seat facing the door. He had the red polo shirt that marked him as an employee of the pizza parlor, and long, stringy brown hair that tumbled down the sides of this face to his shoulders. A short stubbly beard framed his face, and spittle was running down his chin. He was bumping in the bench seat, moving jerkily forward and backward, and his wide eyes were unfocused, staring at the tabletop in front of himself as he mouthed rapid words that Jeff couldn't hear from this distance.

His face was streaked with blood, as were his arms beneath the sleeves of his polo shirt.

The perp, apparently.

Jeff took him in at a glance, but quickly looked back toward the victim, and the patrol Sergeant who was just standing from looking him over.

He was mid-40s, of age with Jeff, and starting to go to fat a bit beneath the crisp blues of his uniform. But his dark grey eyes were were hard, sharp with intelligence beneath the curly black hair on his head.

Sergeant Dearborne nodded greeting as Jeff stepped toward him. "Evening, Detective," Dearborne said. "This is a weird one."

Jeff returned the nod. "What do you have, Tom?"

Dearborne gestured toward the dead man. "Name's Clifford Simek. He's here with his girlfriend," he didn't point toward the sobbing woman, but he didn't need to, "and they're having pizza."

"Shocker."

Dearborne's stoic facade cracked for a second as he raised a wry eyebrow Jeff's way. Jeff just returned it deadpan for a second, and Dearbrone sniffed softly; almost a chuckle.

Almost.

"Anyway, this guy," he pointed at the bobbing guy in the booth, "comes out from the kitchen with that knife. Walks right up and stabs Simek in the chest, cold as ice. Then he just stands there, looking at him as Simek dies."

Jeff waited a couple seconds. Dearborne didn't say anything else, so he made a "get on with it gesture" with his right hand. "Then what?"

Dearborne shrugged. "Nothing. The other customers called 911 and when my guys showed up he was still standing there, just staring at Simek and drooling." He glanced over at the girl. "Before she broke down, she told Hassan the perp said something like 'into below' right before he stabbed Simek."

Jeff frowned, then looked over at the girl. She had not

improved noticeably since he started talking with Dearborne; still obviously in no condition to give a coherent statement.

"How many other people were here?"

"Two other couples on dates," Dearborne said. "Three guys on their own who just came in. One cook, a cashier, and an assistant in the back."

"No manager?"

Dearborne nodded toward the perp. "He's the manager. Jason Linski. Son of the owner, from what the cashier said."

Jeff looked back at the bobbing man in the booth, and spent a bit more time looking him over. He was early 20s, or he had a respectably proficient baby face. Fit enough; not a gym rat but not a couch potato either. Average Joe, basically.

"Has the owner showed up?"

"Out of town until the end of the week," Dearborne replied. "Makinsky called him but got voicemail."

Well, that at least meant Jeff wouldn't have interference with his investigation for a couple days. There would be no trouble getting a warrant for the entire premises; it was a crime scene. But the owner would object to keeping it closed to business longer than absolutely necessary.

Understandable, but Jeff hated artificial deadlines attached to his cases, and especially his crime scenes. He couldn't say for certain, but he had strong suspicion at least three scumbags he had tried to put away had walked because he'd been forced out of the crime scene earlier than he should have been.

Not this time though, hopefully.

Jeff nodded. "What happened to the other witnesses?"

"Took their initial statements, got their information, and sent them home. Told them we'd be in touch in the morning."

Made sense. It was getting on toward ten o'clock. And the security camera Jeff saw in the right front corner of the room would be at least as valuable as anything they had to say.

Jeff pointed toward the girl.

"She's unhurt. Her father's on the way to pick her up. Figured we'd let her go; she's not much good to us the way she is right now."

Jeff nodded agreement. They could always interview her tomorrow. Better a good statement than a hysterical one that the Defense could pick apart for contradictions later on.

Back to the perp; he hadn't moved from his perch on the couch's bench seat except to keep bobbing forward and back. Forward and back.

And was Jeff seeing things, or was it always the exact same distance forward and back?

Weird.

He gestured toward Linski, and Dearborne frowned. "I called psych. They've got some people coming with the coroner's office to take him." He paused, then lowered his voice. "I'll tell you, Jeff, I've never seen a perp like this guy. The things he's babbling?"

Jeff looked back at him and raised an questioning eyebrow. Dearborne shrugged and waved toward the perp with his left hand. "Hear for yourself."

Frowning, Jeff took him up on the offer and walked the few paces over to the booth where Linski sat. The two patrol officers with him perked up a bit as Jeff got closer. The closer one, the younger of the two, with a round dark face and a shaved head that reflected the light from the parlor's overhead lights like a cue-ball, looked at Jeff with a perplexed expression.

"Don't make no sense, Detective," the young patrolman said.

Jeff was about to nod agreement; then he heard the words streaming out of Linski's mouth and realized the patrolman wasn't talking about the crime.

"...from the void to the beyond bless he who walks in the

shadows of the blood and the fist of heaven who comes on the winds of shadow in the sweetness of the sour and the twisting of the straight may he never fail in his oblivion though the winds of time blow to zero and…"

On and on, a stream of words that evoked images in Jeff's mind but no coherent meaning. Just an apparently endless stream of inanity that somehow, almost, touched upon making sense. The kind of sense that made Jeff's mind rebel in even contemplating it.

He had to stop himself from recoiling from the man and the strangely meaningful gibberish he was spewing.

The fist of heaven who comes on the winds of shadow…

Jeff forced himself to stillness, and swallowed. "Has he been like this the whole time?"

Cue-ball nodded, licking his lips. "Pretty much."

"Psych's on the way."

Another nod.

Good.

Dearborne was right. This was a weird one.

Looking at Linski sitting there, bobbing and babbling, Jeff got a crawling sensation up his spine, and he could not entirely suppress a shudder.

A really weird one.

Linski was in a white straight-jacket, sitting Indian-style in his ten by ten padded isolation room with his head resting against the wall's padding so that he was staring, unblinking, up and to the left toward the far corner of the room.

He no longer continued his inane but somehow sensical babble, but his eyes remained unfocused.

But it wasn't like he wasn't seeing something; it was like he was staring, transfixed, at something over in that direction, something that commanded his attention without release.

Jeff left the side of the orderly who had admitted him into the psych holding cell and stepped over to Linski's side.

He didn't respond to Jeff's presence.

Jeff squatted down and bent over to put his head next to Linski's. Then he turned to follow the perp's gaze.

Nothing. Just the seams in the padding where the ceiling met the two adjoining walls in the corner the perp was staring at fixedly.

Jeff stood back up and looked at the orderly, and the Attending Physician who stood behind and to the orderly's right.

The two men could have been made from a mold. Same height; just slightly above average. Some clothing; blue scrubs with ID badges clipped to the left breast. Same pitying yet also condescending expressions on their faces when they looked at Linski.

They varied only in skin tone and hair color. The orderly was pale, ginger. The Attending sub-Saharan black, with curling black hair cut so it only curled out even with his earlobes.

"He's been staring at that same point since he came in?" Jeff asked.

The Attending—Dr. Akawi—nodded. "He only stopped talking about three hours ago. But since then he's been completely silent. And he resists all efforts to feed him or give him water."

Jeff gave a double-take, then looked harder at Akawi. "Come again? He won't let you feed him?"

Akawi shrugged and looked down at Linski. "I misspoke. He doesn't resist. He simply does not cooperate. At all. We give him food, and he does not chew, or swallow. Water, and he lets it overflow his mouth. No attempt at ingestion, at all." Akawi frowned deeply. "It's as though he cannot register what is happening. Or just doesn't care." He lifted his eyes to meet Jeff's. "We will have to resort to intravenous feeding soon, if he does not relent."

Jeff frowned, deeply, then turned to look back at the perp.

He had not budged even a smidgeon of an inch in the time Jeff had been in his padded holding cell.

Not even when Jeff had practically been pressing his head next to his.

Really, really weird.

Tom Dearborne was the supervisor in charge of the patrol team that met Jeff at Linski's apartment to serve the search warrant.

The landlord probably would have let them in without the warrant. From the way he had practically spit on the floor when Jeff mentioned Linski's name; from the way he had not even waited to see the paperwork before he'd opened the locked key storage locker on the wall adjacent to his desk and then led the way up three flights of stairs to the front door of Linski's place; and from the eager gleam in his eyes when Jeff had thanked him for his assistance.

No doubt he would have done it.

But again, the Defense. Jeff had to cross every t, dot every in. So he did.

Not that he needed convincing. He didn't begrudge the defendants their rights. He knew a guys who had been rail-roaded by the same DA Jeff had worked with on a dozen cases or more.

Dude was a scumbag.

But a scumbag representing the people, and no matter

how he had boned Jeff's acquaintance, it was the jury who had handed down the verdict. And that DA had also put hundreds of worse scumbags behind bars where they belonged.

Still, Jeff made a point of not ever crossing the line on interviews or collecting evidence.

Just because the DA was scum didn't mean the rest of the investigation didn't have to be legit. Or at least that's how Jeff saw it.

So he'd spent the ten minutes to write the paperwork and brief the judge to get his search warrant. Really the judge never would have denied it. Not for Linski, not under the circumstances of this case.

And so the landlord let them in, then Dearborne's men made sure all three of the rooms in Linski's apartment were clear, and it was off to work.

It didn't take long to find the smoking gun.

Or...maybe not...

"What the hell is that?" Dearborne said at Jeff's side when the two of them opened the sliding doors of Linski's bedroom closet and looked inside.

Really really weird didn't even begin to cut it.

This was weird times a thousand, squared. Then squared again for good measure.

There were no clothes hanging from the hooks in the closet.

Just a table that had been converted into a makeshift altar, turning the entire closet into a shrine of sorts.

But a shrine to what, Jeff could not figure.

There were strange glyphs painted everywhere on the interior closet walls. Swirling, yet also jagged. Seemingly twisting around themselves into meaningless squiggles but at the same time oddly structured, like if you were looking at it from the precisely right angle it would all make sense.

But not from any angle Jeff could find from within the closet, or from the bedroom outside either.

No matter how he looked at the red and black and green and blue and yellow lines, swirling and jagging and twisting and squaring and breaking around each other, it never became any more clear.

But yet it should have. Part of Jeff's mind knew it had to, and he felt as he looked at it that he was just on the edge of comprehending. If only he could....see...

"Check this out, Detective," Dearborne said, and Jeff jerked back to reality; to the now.

How long had he been staring at those glyphs? How long had he been contemplating the strange pseudo-structure within them?

He glanced down at his watch and saw that only half a minute had passed since they opened the closet doors.

It felt like a short eternity.

Dearborne was bent over the table to Jeff's left, where somehow in his contemplation of the glyphs he had completely missed a leather-bound book, open on a reading pedestal next to half a dozen red wax candles arranged around a pentagram inlaid into the top of the table in paint that looked almost like real silver.

Jeff inched over next to Dearborne and looked down to where the Sergeant's index finger was pointing down onto the text of the book.

The page was yellowed from age, curling slightly at the edge. It was thicker than other kinds of paper Jeff had seen, and rippled and textured almost like leather.

The writing on the page was in a language he didn't know, but it was at the same time smooth and jagged, like the glyphs painted onto the closet walls.

But Jeff didn't need to be able to read the script to decipher the drawing on the open page in front of them. It clearly depicted an altar in a clearing, surrounded by a circle of six cowled figures. A seventh cowled person stood next to the altar with his hands thrown upward to the sky.

An eighth figure was sprawled atop the altar, staring wide-eyed up into the sky above, his jaw slack.

A long, broad-bladed knife was plunged nearly hilt-deep into his chest.

Jeff wasn't a forensics expert, but to his eye it looked to be in exactly the same place the knife had been thrust into Simek's chest back in the pizza parlor.

Jeff breathed out a long, low whistle.

Beside him, Dearborne nodded agreement. He looked side-long at Jeff. "Looks like he was re-enacting the ritual." He paused, then looked back at the book, and shrugged. "Or at least he thought he was. He's clearly bonkers. Maybe he somehow thought his father's pizza place was a hilltop with an altar."

That made sense. Kind of. But also, it was a stretch. Linski was clearly out of it now, but could he really have been that far gone at the time of the murder that he really didn't know he wasn't in a pizza parlor, but a clearing in the middle of a forest?

That seemed a stretch.

And anyway, it was a stretch that would just put him into an insane asylum, instead of prison.

An asylum is worse than prison, a not-so-quiet part of Jeff's mind replied.

And true enough. But that would also mean declaring him legally not guilty due to insanity. And Jeff rebelled against letting a murderer escape even that small amount of account-ability for his crime.

"There has to be more to it," Jeff said.

Dearborne continued looking at him for a second, then shrugged. "You say so. I'll check the rest of the room."

He turned away and walked over to Linski's dresses, on the other side of the room from the closet.

That left Jeff alone with the book, and the altar setup.

He just looked at the strangely-almost-leather pages and the flowing script on them for a moment. And again he felt drawn into those weird designs. Something pulled at him. Bidding him to look deeper. Closer.

Turn the page. See the next secret.

Instead, Jeff turned to the page before the one Linski had been reading.

Just more flowing and graceful but jagged and harsh script, pointing toward something half-seen yet totally hidden.

He turned backwards again. And stopped, shock paralyzing his muscles into complete immobility so that he could not even breath for a second that stretched into ten and then fifteen before he finally was able to force himself to expel the breath he had been holding without even realizing it.

He inhaled then. Loudly. Loudly enough that from the corner of his eye he saw Dearborne stiffen and then spin toward him, the Sergeant's hand coming to rest instinctively on the grip of his weapon, holstered on his belt.

Jeff didn't bother with explanations. He just gestured forcefully for Dearborne to come back over to him.

"What - ?" The question died on Dearborne's lips when he saw the drawing on the page Jeff had turned to.

It couldn't have been the same thing. The book was obviously hundreds of years old. At least. So whoever had drawn this image into it could not have intentionally made it match so exactly.

But nevertheless, there it was. In the book two page-turns back from the drawing of the sacrifice.

A furnace. Or some equivalent. But whatever it was, it was the exact replica of the wood-fired oven in Linski's pizza parlor.

As before, the diagram seemed to grab at Jeff, and it was with no small amount of effort that he forced his eyes away, to look Dearborne in the face.

"We need to get back there. Have a look at that thing."

The Sergeant nodded.

"And we're bringing this with us," Jeff added, by instinct, placing his hand down atop the strange book.

Dearborne paused, hesitating plainly as his instinct to preserve the scene and maintain the integrity of evidence clashed with something else—something primal, almost spiritual; a desire, a need, a nigh-irresistible drawing to see, to know that Jeff could see and fully relate to.

After a second that felt an eternity, Dearborne nodded.

Jeff closed the book, and they left with it.

———

The pizza parlor was still taped off when Jeff and Dearborne arrived. They drove separately, since it would have been a pain to bring Dearborne back to his supervisor cruiser at Linski's; and anyway he might get a call while they were at the parlor.

Dearborne looked surprised when they came to the door and found it taped off, though. "I thought it had been released already?"

Jeff flashed a grin at him. "Technically yes. But Mr. Linski doesn't get back til midnight, and he won't be able to open it until tomorrow afternoon no matter what, so I had them leave the tape up. Just in case."

Jeff pulled the tape off from the front door and pushed it open, and stepped inside. He could feel Dearborne hesitate in following. Driven by disapproval?

Didn't matter; there was nothing illegal about what Jeff had done. Not technically, anyway. So they were clear. For now at least.

Good thing too. If they'd discovered the book and altar even just a few hours later, it would have been a heck of a pain to explain to the elder Linski, let alone to a judge, why they needed to get back inside to search. Again.

Just as well it wasn't needed.

The inside of the parlor was dark, fitting for the growing darkness of afternoon fading into evening combined with the fact that the lights were all turned off.

But dark as it was, it was still somehow infused with a kind of light, so Jeff found he could almost see normally. It was like being in a room with lights on a dimmer that had been turned down to just above their fully dark setting, so a person could see everything but not be entirely sure that he could.

Part of Jeff's mind—a large part— told him to just hit the light switch to the left of the door as he stepped inside.

But somehow, for some reason that made sense even though it was ludicrous, he reasoned it would be better to not do that right now.

After all, he could see. And they didn't need light for what they had come to complete, did they?

Wait....complete?

"My God," Dearborne said, from Jeff's left.

He looked at the Sergeant and saw that Dearborne's gaze was fixed toward the rear of the parlor, past the countertop toward the work and serving spaces back there.

Now Jeff realized there was more light coming from back there. And yet as he glanced to his right, then back toward the door he saw that the light did not illuminate anything.

To either side of himself and behind it was all twilight gloom going into full dark, no matter that he could see.

Looking back forward again, though...

Ahead, vision was clear, and complete. A dark not-light that nevertheless revealed all shown forth, now clearly coming from something to the right of the oven, on the work counters Jeff had seen in his initial survey of the scene seemingly an eternity ago, even though it had been less than two days since then.

Dearborne had started moving forward, toward the gap to the left of the service counter that led into the kitchen areas.

Jeff followed, because that was why they had come, after all.

When he passed the counter, it seemed that the space shifted somehow. Where he knew the kitchen area was relatively small; enough so that the cashier plus cook plus assistant accounted for all of the people who could comfortably be back there under normal circumstances, now it seemed that the length of space from where he was to the oven ahead must be nearly a hundred feet. And over to the work counters on the right half that.

Jeff's mind rejected that idea; he clearly had memory of this space being much smaller.

But his perception could not deny it. The size of the space; its feeling of immensity. It overwhelmed his memory's protest.

A new scent was on the air, different that the scents of baking and pizza and merriment that he knew before. Now if was sharper, tangy, but also rank like something that should be good lingered here but had become rotten.

The not-light grew stronger, shining an orange-green tint on the scene that was even now morphing before Jeff's eyes.

The kitchen apparatus was fading; the counter behind losing reality, fading into mist.

The oven remained; the actuation mechanism to light its fire on the wall next to it as well solid in its reality.

The work counter as well, though its white top was shifting into grey-blue, almost like stone of its own.

There was something lying atop the counter. Something paler. But Jeff couldn't make it out.

Dearborne walked over to the lighting mechanism next to the oven—somehow covering a hundred feet in a single pace—and flipped the switch. The oven came to life, an internal fire leaping up from the burner within to shrieks that almost sounded like men and women screaming that suddenly echoed in Jeff's mind.

He stumbled backward, losing grip on the book as he reflexively pressed his palms to his ears, the shrieks were so loud.

Dearborne crossed the distance back in another step and stopped, looking at Jeff quizzically.

"You ok, Detective?" he said.

He sounded his normal self, but his face was twisting. Like bubbles flowing beneath his flesh were running up one side of his head and down the other. His skin grew more pink, than red.

And when he smiled, his eyes flashed red for a second.

The a second later he was back to his normal self. The same man Jeff had worked with, gotten a drink with, for almost twenty years.

"Tom - " Jeff tried to say, but found it only came out in a croak. Like his vocal chords could not bear to give voice to thoughts he couldn't begin to put in order.

Dearborne smiled at him. "It's all good, Jeff," he said, and bent down to pick up the book.

"Linski botched the ceremony," he continued as he straightened, and there was an undertone to his voice that Jeff could not place his finger on.

Dearborne was always more bass than baritone, but now there were throbbing levels even below that. Levels that Jeff could feel but not hear; levels that impacted on his very mind, and he felt a rising revulsion tinged with terror.

Yet at the same time he found himself petrified to the spot;

stuck the same way he had been when he examined the glyphs in Linski's closet. Something about the new deeper resonances of Dearborne's voice reflected and harmonized and combined and opposed and reinforced each other and created a dissonant harmony that reverberated through Jeff's very soul so he could only stand there gaping at the ugly, abhorrent and yet completely inescapably sublime repellent beauty of each word as Dearborne stepped closer to the counter.

"The sacrifice cannot be consummated until the vessel is complete," Dearborne said. And not Dearborne, as once again Jeff got a flash of something else—some alien thing bubbling beneath the man, working to overwhelm the Sergeant and burst through into being of its own.

But yet it couldn't. That insight flashed through Jeff's being in a heartbeat as the truth of it reverberated from the intonation of the thing within Dearborne's words.

Not without completion; until then it was trapped.

"You can I can complete the work though," Dearborne said, and picked up the object that had been lying on the countertop.

He turned back toward Jeff, and his eyes were fully red now. Red, and hot; Jeff felt the heat of his gaze as Dearborne turned.

Or maybe it was just the heat of the oven. Jeff couldn't be sure.

He was sure about the thing in Dearborne's right hand, though. Not a butcher knife like Linski had used on his customer. A broad-bladed dagger like the one in the drawing Jeff had found within the book.

The book! Where was -

There, he saw it, atop the counter where Dearborne had placed it to take up the dagger. And it was glowing with the same not-light that had lit the place up when they walked in.

The same, and yet dim; a shadow of the shadowy light that was already shining. Like it was the junior partner.

Jeff's eyes moved up the wall from the counter and saw the source, the thing that had produced the not-light to begin with.

Long and flat, in a cooling rack above the counter. Flat, and round, it glowed in that dark light, brighter and yet devoid of brightness so that Jeff could not bear to look at it at first. But after a few blinks to clear the intensity he saw the light wasn't coming from the entire disk, but from a dozen or more smaller pieces atop the disk.

As his eyes and mind opened to that fact, he realized what he was looking at, and the absurdity of it took him aback.

"Wait. Tom...the vessel is the pizza?"

Dearborne paused, looked back at the disk, and the objects atop it. The red of his eyes flickered, then resumed, and a twisted smile appeared on his face. "Do you still not see?"

Then he was across the space between them and he had his left hand around Jeff's throat.

It was like being in a vice; the iron strength of his fingers betrayed any hope of ever considering breaking his grip.

Dearborne—of the thing that inhabited what once had been Dearborne—pulled his face close to itself, and Jeff gasped as the sudden pain from the scorching heat of its breath.

"Fool," it said.

Then it flung Jeff away, its fingers around his throat picking him up until he left his feet. He flew across the space until he struck something solid and landed on his side, atop the counter beneath the cooling rack.

The rest of the space was now completely red-orange mist, except for the oven at what had been the rear. Whatever coolness of evening had faded between a dry heat that was growing more oppressive by the moment.

The pleasant scents of the pizza parlor replaced by sulfur and dirt smoke, rot and decay.

Hauntingly dark melody gone, replaced only by mournful groans and screams, but screams that somehow had a measure of ecstasy intermixed with their agony.

All twisted, all wrong. All beautiful, all enticing.

Jeff lay on his side and groaned, trying to wrap his mind around what was happening and failing. Trying to figure out to survive and not wanting too. Struggling to comprehend and finding at the end of that road a void and a blackness and a dark light and a consumption and an eternity piled upon infinity piled until universes consumed by nothingness overarched by a cold and meaningless lack of anything resembling thought or caring or desire, just an all-sucking singularity that consumed everything and produced everything and left nothing remaining but insanity and gifted nothing that was love but also yearned and hungered for nothingness that was the only thing that could feed it as it swelled into immensity but shrank into oblivion at the same time and...

Jeff realized he was screaming. Screaming at the immensity, the nothingness, the implacableness, the weakness of it all.

It was everything he could ever conceive and nothing, and then something was rolling him onto his back.

Red eyes in the face that once had been Dearborne looked down at him, and he saw the broad-bladed knife rising.

"Blood for the sauce, sauce for the goose, goose for the pie, pie for the stomach, stomach for the body, and growth for the new beast. The beast that will consume all." Dearborne's voice wasn't something Jeff heard; it throbbed through his body, echoed through his mind.

And the blade reached its apex. It hovered, and began to plunge toward Jeff's chest.

The light-that-was-not glinted off the cutting edges of the

knife, flashed from its tip, and Jeff tried to recoil away from it even as he arched his torso upward to meet it.

He fled, and he ran forward, and in his motions his hand came to rest on something had on his right hip.

His sidearm.

Instinct for life struggled again the blessed curse of the sirens calling him down into eternity tortured oblivion, and the joy that never-ending suffering would bring as his sanity drained into insanity that bread new understanding.

Somehow, somewhere his pistol came up, and real light shattered the light-that-was-not once. Twice. Three times.

Dearborne's eyes widened. Flashed to white. Then he fell onto his back on the ground, the knife scattering away from his limp grasp.

Jeff pushed himself up, and the oven was still firing. The pie above still glowing.

And he knew what he had to do.

Leaving his pistol behind, he reached up and took the disk.

Stumbled over to the edge of the oven.

And tossed the disk within.

Reality erupted into fire and light—real light. A titanic impact to his chest sent him stumbling backward, and he struck something hard.

Light—white and true but also red-orange as the not-light fought against it—scoured his being, and his mind opened to shades of color he never conceived of before. Flashed of flavor that fried his tongue for the blasphemy of even conceiving of them.

Knowledge that spanned all eternity and the infinite expanse of existence collided with his mind, and he screamed.

He screamed long and long, until he could hear no more.

Then blackness claimed him, and he knew only a cursed and blessed oblivion.

His orderly led the way to Holding Cell Number 4, and Doctor Akami had to fight back annoyance at the man's slow pace.

But he could not scold the man; not today, in front of his visitors.

Akami looked back at the half dozen faces following them, influential and brilliant minds from the foremost institutes of psychiatric research, and felt a warm glow of pride within himself.

The most imminent minds of his profession, come to see his unique patient. Hear of Akami's diagnosis and his methods of treatment for this most unusual case. After this, Akami would be able to write his own ticket, wherever he went.

Finally, they stopped at the small window looking into the padded holding cell, and Akami stepped to the side, gesturing toward the window for his visitors to look in.

"Detective Jeffrey Mosby. Formerly a well-decorated police officer, committed here after murdering one of his fellow officers in cold blood and burning down an entire city block in the worst case of arson this State has seen in fifty years."

He went on to describe the symptom's of Mosby's affliction, what led him to make his diagnosis, and his visitors gave him due attention.

Within, the patient sat in a straight jacket, his legs tucked Indian-style and his head lolling back so it rested against the padding of the wall and his eyes fixed on a point at the far corner of the ceiling.

He focused on something no one else could see; stared at it unblinking.

His mouth moved, and soft words came out, almost too soft to hear.

"...bless he who walks in the shadows of the blood and the

fist of heaven who comes on the winds of shadow in the sweetness of the sour and the twisting of the straight may he never fail in his oblivion though the winds..."

After several minute, Akami and his companions walked away, to the next patient, though they wouldn't care about that one.

And Jeff remained.

Somewhere.

CROWNED EMPEROR

Along with the Icaran Confederation Navy, the other science fiction setting I revisit often is the Qorathi Empire. They're actually located in the same universe, though they don't know each other...yet.

The Qorathi Empire came first, with my novella Veritas Morte, which introduced Prince Lucien. My concept for Lucien went like this: What if Prince Lotor, from Voltron, didn't realize he was the crown prince of an evil empire? And what would happen when he found out?

That first novella deals with that process of discovery. This story picks up a little bit later, on his coronation day.

Enjoy!

The crown that now marked him as Emperor, and Protector of the Chosen, was only a few tens of grams of platinum mixed with silver. Lucien Bandemyr knew this.

But when the High Priest placed it atop his head during the culminating moment of his coronation ceremony—when he officially took on responsibility for guiding and protecting the lives and fortunes of the hundreds of millions of people on the three dozen worlds that made up the Qorathi Empire—it felt as though it weighed ten times that.

A hundred.

The High Priest's words washed over him, but he barely heard. Not that he needed to; the words were rote ritual, used for a century or more and well-known by everyone in the Imperial Court.

Still, it struck Lucien that he really ought to pay more attention, out of respect if nothing else.

Strange how that consideration weighed so heavily on his mind. A few months ago he wouldn't have been concerned about whether or not he had shown the proper respect for the elderly priest, even if only within the confines of his own head.

He was the High Priest, certainly, but his origin was lowly: the fifth son of a minor house six jumps from Qora that Lucien only knew of because he had been forced to learn every house in the Empire. Not because they actually amounted to anything.

Not so long ago, Lucien would have had trouble separating the man's lofty position from that lowly beginning.

Before the campaign in the Neonovus System, and Minister Ymmerson's betrayal, and the revelation of his own father's sins as a result.

Now he couldn't help but think perhaps people from the lower ranks more worthy of respect and attention. Or perhaps just that trusting and respecting them held less danger than the higher houses.

Foolishness; he couldn't just cast aside the great Houses, and with them all the ministers and functionaries who made the Empire's apparatus function, if not smoothly at least without too terribly much strain.

But as he walked from the throne room in the Imperial Palace on Qora, for once not even noticing the crystalline ceiling resting apparently weightlessly atop the lofty fluted columns that lined the sides of the chamber, or the pinkish-blue sky and puffy white clouds floating past in the sky above, he could not put that thought from his mind.

Abernathy, his long-time teacher and advisor, dressed as always in his cowled grey robes that matched the hair on his head and the beard that lined his chin, walked beside him and half a pace behind to his right. His honor guard—Marines in full formal regalia—led the way. And his train of functionaries and lesser advisors followed.

And he felt alone.

It had been a long four months since he had called an end to the Corellis campaign, ceasing the fighting in the Neonovus system, after his father's death. Four months that had been filled full.

Preparations for his father's funeral and internment. Dealing with the legalities of dividing the late Emperor Archibald's personal estate between Lucien and his sister, Emilia, and her husband, Count Poterick of Heaven's Gate. Re-staffing the Ministries, especially in light of Ymmerson's treachery, to ensure the loyalty of the new Ministers. Planning for the coronation. And now the coronation ceremony itself.

Four months that passed in a flash, and with seemingly not a moment to just think and absorb all that had happened during that time.

Now it was done, and Lucien was Emperor.

And as he passed through corridors that Lucien knew so well on his way to the grand hall where the post-coronation feast was to be held, corridors he had run through and played in as a child and then later walked as a young man so that they were as natural and familiar to him as his own body, he noted not a one of them.

His entire mind roiled with uncertainty and doubt—doubt that he could not let intrude onto the mask of calm assurance that he put on for others to see.

He was not ready for this. He had not yet reached his twentieth year, had not thought to take the throne for decades yet. No one had ever sat on the throne of Qora at such a young age as he.

He was not ready, and yet here he was.

Could he even do this?

Or would he end up a footnote in history? Lucien the Fallen, whose failure presaged the downfall of the Empire into competing and warring satrapies, easy prey for the surrounding powers to snap up.

Powers like the Tsago Dominace, who had taken Hazador mere weeks before his father's death at Ymmerson's hand.

He saw Abernathy looking sidelong at him as they walked together, a little bubble between the two of them and the rest of his entourage. Still, his teacher's words were hushed, barely carrying to Lucien's ears; Abernathy knew better than Lucien even how an idle word could reach an enemy's ear.

"One step at a time, your Majesty."

The words struck through the doubt flooding Lucien's mind like a rapier thrust with expert aim, though the tone was warm, almost companionable.

It broke Lucien's dour reverie, reminding him that he at

least wasn't completely alone. There was one man who would always have his back.

Lucien flashed him a quick smile and a nod, and Abernathy returned the nod.

Moments later they entered the reception hall.

Lucien had waited in the throne room for the others who filed over and got situated as the director of ceremonies and protocol dictated, so that he would be the last to enter. As was fitting.

Still he had a wait at the tall black-stained double doors that lead into the reception hall. Two attendants in the formal livery of Imperial chattel, one for each half of the door, stood waiting with their hands on the doorknobs, their heads turned toward the side where one of the protocol director's assistants, clad in a white kimono with a blue sash, waited with his left index finger pressed to his ear, to a communication bud worn there no doubt.

His eyes, grey-brown beneath a shortly-cut red-brown hair, met Abernathy's for a moment. Abernathy's questioning expression elicited a raised finger from his right hand, as though to say, "One moment."

That moment stretched into a smaller eternity, and Lucien was tempted to shout at him to get on with it. But right then he perked up and looked away from Abernathy to the servants at the doors. He nodded, and they pulled the door open, toward Lucien and his entourage.

The room beyond was smaller than a stranger to Qora would have thought it would be, considering the size of the empire and its wealth. Maybe fifty meters on a side and seven or eight meters high. It was made from pinkish-grey stone that had been carved into fluted columns at intervals along its walls, supporting a vaulted ceiling that was painted with murals of glorious scenes from Qora's past, going all the way back to the time of the split with old Terra, now long forgotten in the murky past.

Starships and hard men abounded in those murals, hard men who had the same slightly hooked nose as Lucien and his late father, who all wore their hair in the style of the crown: closely-cropped at the sides and top but left to grow long in the rear.

Lucien's hair followed his father's black curls, but not all of his ancestors' did. A few were blond. One was a redhead. But the cut of their hair, so severe and yet almost undisciplined in the way that long tail flowed, was all the same.

A mark of Lucien's office even without the silver-platinum diadem now adorning his forehead.

The room was lit by dangling chandeliers made of gold, each of them holding half a dozen light elements on long curved arms that cast a uniform, warm glow throughout the space.

Dozens of round tables set for twelve stood arranged in evenly-spaced rows, topped by charcoal-grey tablecloths that matched the uniform Lucien wore. The rows ended at the royal purple carpeting that stretched from Lucien's doorway to the raised dais on the far side of the room, on which a long VIP table stood, adorned with a tablecloth of the same shade.

Lucien's destination.

The attendees of the feast were all standing behind their assigned seats. Many of the men in the crowd were dressed in military attire like Lucien's, except that while he bore the Imperial Purple in the sash that went from his shoulder to hip their sashes depicted their branch of service: sky blue for the Fleet, crimson for the Marines, deep green for regular Army, and yellow for Air and Space forces.

Others wore the blue formal kimonos of the Imperial Court. A few toward the edges of the room wore white, matching the protocol man's inside the doorway; lower-level personnel in the various ministries who still had somehow managed to rate an invitation to the event.

The women in the crowd wore gowns that varied as much as the women themselves varied from each other. Demure—usually on the older ladies—all the way down to almost slinky on some of the younger, in all shades of the color spectrum. Except purple.

As the doors finished swinging open, a fanfare of trumpets sounded from unseen speakers, and Lucien's Marine escort marched forward in unison, their boots marking time in measured unity as they dispersed along the carpeting from the door to the VIP table, pairs of the liveried men stopping at intervals along the way so that the cohort ended up lining the entire route Lucien was to take.

Then they turned as one, facing each other crisply and bringing the silver-polished repeating rifles each had born at port arms down into a stiff and uniform present arms, in a single movement that halted as quickly as it began.

The anthem of the Empire, strings accompanied with a throbbing bass drum with a single trumpet carrying the melody, began playing, and Lucien walked down the line of stony-faced Marines to the place prepared for him.

Abernathy followed, as before at his side and slightly behind.

The rest of entourage waited.

He felt the eyes of the waiting hundreds following him as he walked, his shoulders back and his head high in the marching gait he had learned almost before he learned how to read, his expression as stiff and imperially regal as he could force it to be beneath the weight of those stares.

How many of this group secretly wished for his failure? How many would give honest support? How many simply did not care except to the extent that it would affect their own petty fortunes one way or the other?

Far too many of the later, Lucien knew from a lifetime observing the goings-on at court.

Far too few of the second.

And as to the first, though his spies knew of some plots, and some rumors of plots, it was impossible to tell for certain.

It sent a shiver up his spine.

The VIP table was full, the assigned guests waiting behind their chairs for Lucien to sit first. He recognized the heads of the various ministries and Lord Morsy, his Chamberlain, as well as heads of the military branches.

Emilia and her husband, a man ten years her senior who was starting to go grey at the temple, sat to the left of Lucien's seat. Her gown was imperial grey with a purple sash about the waist. Her curly black hair, the same shade as Lucien's, hung loosely about her shoulders and she she beamed a smile when their eyes met.

Count Poterick's nod when Lucien looked from his sister to him was perfectly formal and proper, but Lucien thought he saw a flash of warmth in his eyes for a second that came close to matching Emilia's. His kimono was the standard blue of the Court but boasted a broach on his left breast showing a shining sun above a closed set of golden gates, the sigil of his star system.

Diplomats from the surrounding powers sat farther out along the table. His eyes lingered for a longer moment than he had intended on one of them in particular.

She was tall for a woman, and slender but curvy, in a modestly-cut gown of deep scarlet that was tantalizing for all that it was the epitome of good taste. Her hair was black at the roots and down the sides of her face, but dyed to grey and then scarlet to match her dress at the ends. Her eyes flashed with intelligence, and when they met his her lips turned upward ever so slightly in greeting.

Ophelia Temisen, princess of the Capestrani Republic.

Lucien knew she would be here in her parents' place, and he had both looked forward to and dreaded seeing her again.

He forced his eyes away and looked to her right, where at the end of the table the former Prime Minister of the Free Republic of Hazador stood in a dark blue suit of republican cut and a thin silver-grey necktie. His dark eyes were sunken, like he had not been getting much sleep. And Lucien couldn't blame him. He had been working tirelessly to try to get assistance for his people, a diaspora of refugees now scattered throughout the Empire and some of the other surrounding systems.

He had also been lobbying hard for the Empire to assist them in re-taking their system, and from the frank and not-so-friendly way he returned Lucien's look he didn't appreciate the no's Lucien's father had sent through channels.

And the same no's Lucien had continued to send since his father's death.

At the opposite end of the table from Hazador sat the Ambassador from the Tsago Dominace and his wife. He had on a green high-collared silk coat that was embroiled with golden dragons around the collar and the cuffs of his sleeves. Her dress was silk, and matched his shade for shade. His head was bald, his goatee deep black, and he had the angular eyes that shouted his Han bloodline even if his status as a high-level representative of the Dominance wouldn't have made that obvious.

Hazador and the Dominance were a powder keg even being in the same room together, but there had been no good way to not invite either of them.

As Lucien rounded the table, passing the Dominance's Ambassador on his way to his chair in the center, he couldn't help but think they should have found a way, and no matter if it ruffled Hazador's feathers.

Dinner was sumptuous: five courses beginning with a spiced duck soup, followed with a salad of greens dressed with a raspberry vinaigrette, then chicken and beef in a reduction sauce that somehow managed to bring out each meat's separate flavors without overpowering either of them. Then more greens atop a mash of some sort that Lucien couldn't identify but left his tongue reeling from sweet to hot back to sweet again.

And then cheesecake topped with cherry sauce; Lucien's favorite dessert from when he was a young boy.

Fortunately, there were to be no speeches this evening.

There was to be dancing, however. And by tradition Lucien was expected to give time to all comers of appropriate rank. Very quickly he found himself swept up in dance after dance with one young lady of the court after another.

One and all were winsome, if not all beautiful, and all were obviously trying to court his favor.

Lucien couldn't blame them; he was unmarried, not even engaged. Every family in the Empire would want to pair a daughter with him if they could manage it.

Politics.

As he was dancing with one dark-skinned girl, the third daughter of House Mennil, Lucien flashed back to one of the last conversations he had had with his father, the morning Emperor Archibald had been poisoned.

The Emperor had revealed he had been considering arranging a marriage between Lucien and Ophelia Temisen, and Lucien had rebelled against the thought.

He looked into young Miss Mennil's face as they danced—she was probably two years younger than him, so just past her ascendance—and saw past the friendly and respectful smile on her face to the trepidation in her eyes that she almost but not quite managed to bury beneath a noble facade. And he wanted to tell her he knew exactly how she felt.

He could not of course.

They all had to play their games of decorum.

In point of fact, she was rather pretty. Lucien was certain she'd have no end of suitors that she actually wanted.

Their dance ended and he retreated a half-step, bowing from the waist. "Thank you, Miss Mennil."

She smiled at him—and this time it was fully genuine—as she curtsied. "Your Majesty," she said, then she turned to go.

Relieved, no doubt, to be done with it.

Lucien sighed and turned around. And found himself face to face with Ophelia Temisen.

Her eyes were twinkling. With amusement, or something else? There could be layers to her that were hard to read; he had learned that well enough during their first meeting.

Ophelia didn't bother with a curtsy, just stretched her arms out into a dancing pose. "May I, your Majesty?" Her tone was completely proper, her smile friendly. But Lucien sensed some teasing there as well.

Or maybe something else.

He stepped forward as the band began their next song, taking her right hand in his left and placing his right hand on her hip. "My pleasure, your Highness," he said, and she laughed.

As they moved across the dance floor, passing a mass of other dancing couples, she glanced left then right and her smile grew a bit more broad. "Everyone's watching, you know."

He snorted softly, and bent forward to place her into a dip. "Of course," he said, "you have a reputation for trouble."

She laughed again as she straightened. "That's not it." Her eyebrows rose. "The handsome young emperor. Unmarried, and ripe for the snatching up." That twinkle just intensified, and the teasing was plain now. "Every powerful family in your Empire is aching to get their daughter's hooks into you."

That she was paralleling his thoughts from just a moment ago somehow was completely unsurprising.

"The Emperor must do his duty for the Empire," he said, keeping his tone polite and friendly and not taking her bait. He sent her into a slow spin, then stepped in to catch her at the end of it. "Secure an heir, and all that."

"Of course." She pursed her lips, looking thoughtful for a moment, then gave a little toss of her head, making her colorful hair flare out in time with their bodies as he guided her into a turn.

"You know, my parents thought about trying to pair us up," she said after a short while longer, and Lucien almost lost his footing from the shock.

A lifetime of training helped him recover almost as soon as the moment took him, but she noticed. Of course she did. That teasing smile returned again, and the twinkle in her eyes expanded still further.

"What better way to make sure your big mighty empire doesn't gobble little us up?" She said it light-heartedly, but he knew that was a very real concern for her Republic.

And not just hers.

"I told them not to bother," she added after a second, as they pulled apart and released hands for a moment. "You are not your father."

Six months ago that would have stung—enraged him. But he knew the truth of how his father had manipulated and conquered his neighbors, the ruthless tactics he had used to do so.

Another thing he had learned from Neonovus.

It still wasn't something he liked to hear though.

He stepped back into her and turned her to the left, not

trusting himself to reply for the moment.

"And besides," Ophelia said, and her smile turned from teasing to sly. "I reminded them you'd already met me. And that was enough to convince them the chance was already ruined."

Whatever bite her comment about his father had made, Lucien found himself laughing out loud at that.

The song ended shortly after that, and he stepped back from her. He wasn't at all surprised to find he had legitimately enjoyed their dance.

Or to see that she had as well.

"Thank you for the dance, your Majesty," she said. And did curtsy then.

"Your Highness," he said, bowing in return.

Next followed a string of young maidens from more Houses than he cared to count. A few were charming. One was quite striking. But they became a blur so that he found himself almost dancing on autopilot. Repeating the same answers to the same questions from different mouths.

And becoming dreadfully bored.

So it came as a bit of a relief when Emilia left Poterick's side to take a turn with her little brother.

They were silent for a little while; he just looked at her.

It appeared she had healed from the shock of their father's death. At least somewhat.

Poterick had reported that the news had very nearly crushed her, that she had become despondent, not eating and barely sleeping for weeks.

Lucien was six years younger than her, but he remembered how Emperor Archibald had doted on her. Whereas Lucien was the heir, to be molded and forged into the man to rule the empire after he was gone, Emilia was his prize. And she had loved Archibald far more deeply than Lucien imagined he ever could have.

It was more than a father's love for a daughter, Lucien supposed. Looking at Emilia now as she moved with him across the floor, he was struck by how much she resembled their late mother.

Especially as she grew ill, and after she passed, it must have felt to Archibald like Emilia was a lifeline to the woman he once knew and loved.

Or maybe Lucien was just speculating.

Regardless, though he could still see pain in Emilia's eyes, she hid it well beneath outward happiness for him. So it was an improvement.

"You looked like you enjoyed your time with Princess Ophelia," she said all of a sudden, and he blinked at her in surprise.

For a moment, that hidden sorrow fled completely beneath amusement as she leaned in slightly. "You should have heard Lady Telemunde gripe about it. She wants her Cybeline to nab you, you know." She raised an eyebrow at him.

Lucien had to hold back a shudder. Of all the maidens he had danced with, Cybeline had stood out as the most attractive, but also most unpleasant of the bunch.

"No chance of that," he said. Firmly.

Emilia chuckled. "I assumed as much."

A minute later he spun her, and when they came back together in a close part of the dance, she leaned in, and her tone became soft but insistent. "Poterick says all is in readiness."

Lucien nodded, and his mind went into overdrive.

He had promised himself to change the direction his father had turned the Empire toward. To deal more honorably with the other powers, and with his people. But Archibald had been steering his course for decades, and righting a ship of the Empire's size would not be easy.

Lucien had approached Poterick with the first set of reforms he intended to make after taking the crown, with the hope the Count could help line up support within the noble houses so his initiatives would not be dead on arrival.

He might be Emperor, but his word would matter little if no one would actually follow through with his orders.

That Poterick had been successful meant that the initial pieces Lucien needed to commence his work were ready.

Just in time.

Lucien looked over toward the VIP table where most of his ministers still sat, talking amongst each other.

If all went well, these next few months would see many of their worlds upended. And they would not be happy about it. Some of them. Maybe most of them.

Hopefully some would see past their own self-interest to the greater good his new policies would create for the Empire and its people.

It was going to be a fight, either way.

"Thank him for me," he said, and Emilia nodded.

She looked like she was going to say something else for a second. Then the moment passed and she nodded again.

Then the song was over, and it was back to the stream of maidens.

Lucien sighed inwardly, but kept up appearances. And did manage to have a bit of fun here and there.

All the same, as the evening drew to a close, he was happy to be done.

Abernathy walked at his side as he strode down the corridors toward the Emperor's apartments—his apartments—on the other side of the palace from the reception hall. A pair of Marine guards led the way a few meters ahead, and another pair trailed.

"Poterick's ready to go," Lucien said to his teacher, and Abernathy nodded.

"Then all is in place," Abernathy said. He paused. "Are you sure you want to take this course?"

Lucien scowled at him. "We've discussed this, Abernathy."

"I know, your Majesty. But once you've begun it will be too late to reconsider. If you have any doubt—"

"None."

Abernathy returned his look in silence for a moment, then nodded. "I will put the word out."

"Good."

Ahead, the corridor turned to the right. Twenty meters further along would be the door to his apartments. And rest.

Lucien could hardly wait.

"It looked like Princess Ophelia was pleased to see you again."

Lucien stopped.

It took Abernathy two paces to realized he had. The old man turned to look back at him with an eyebrow raised. "Your majesty?"

"Don't you start on that too, Abernathy. I had to hear about it from Emilia already. Last thing I need is *two* women gossiping at me about her."

Abernathy's lips twitched into a half-smile, half-smirk for a second. "She is an impressive young lady, your Majesty. You could do much worse."

Lucien just stared at him.

After a moment, Abernathy's reserve cracked, and he let out a little chuckle, then nodded his head. "As you wish."

"Thank you."

But as he closed the door to his apartments, Lucien could swear he could still hear Abernathy chuckling as he walked away to his own quarters.

Lucien groaned.

MISS MELODY AND THE JAIL CELL

Miss Melody's Cafe is a warm, welcoming, mystical place that serves food for the body, healing for the soul, and appears anywhere souls have need. But only once, and only when the need is great.

This is the fourth story I've written featuring Miss Melody, and there will be many more to come, I'm sure.

Enjoy!

T he Uber came to a halt in front of the James County Courthouse, and for a moment Timothy just looked out at it through the window.

A solid mass of grey concrete, with severe lines and tiny slivers of windows that stacked atop each other like the wounds from some great claw that had been dragged down across the face of the cubic building.

It was colorless, bleak, ugly, and uninviting.

A fitting place to house the mockery of justice that was our modern system.

He swallowed, adjusting the blue and white tie he wore beneath a cheap navy-blue sports coat. He didn't have the rest of the suit to go with it, so he had on dark blue jeans and a white collared shirt; fortunately the sports coats concealed the shirt's short sleeves.

He watched as people streamed up the half-dozen concrete stairs leading up to the courthouse's main entrance. Many of them appeared to be lawyers, in slick tailored suits with brief-cases in their hands and cell phones to their heads. Others were average Joes and Janes like Tim, hoping to escape the clutches of the system with freedom and at least some small amount of cash left in the bank.

After the vultures feasted on their accounts.

Well, Tim thought after a moment, not completely like him. He wasn't in danger of going away to a cell for years; that was his brother. But Tim's bank account had felt the pecking none-theless.

"We're here, buddy," said the driver from the front seat. He was early middle-aged, with friendly blue eyes and a close-cropped blond beard, starting to go grey, that matched the curly hair atop his head.

Tim turned to look at him and found that friendliness still

there, but there was an insistence about his demeanor now. A "get out, I got things to do" feel.

Tim couldn't blame him; another pickup request had come in two blocks ago and the guy wasn't out here taking schlubs like him around for his health.

Money to be made, and all that.

Still, for a couple seconds he felt a flash of anger at the man, like he was forcing Tim into the inferno that just might burn away everything he had known in his life to this point.

He almost lashed out, but he stopped himself. Not the guy's fault Sam had done what he had.

So instead, he nodded, said a quick "Thanks," then got out.

The Uber sped off almost as soon as he closed the car door behind himself, and Tim wished he could be within it.

Sentencing was today, and he feared it was going to be bad. Looking up at the court building, Tim wondered if he would ever see his brother alive and free again after today.

There was some hope; Sam had never been in trouble before. Still...

The scene around him dimmed noticeably, and though he knew it was just a cloud passing in front of the sun, Tim felt a shiver of dread pass up his spine. Like that cloud had been God's confirmation of every fear Tim was harboring right then.

The moment passed, and Tim had to inhale deeply to suppress the shiver that wanted to become physical.

Man up, he told himself. It might not be that bad.

He didn't really believe it, but he squared his shoulders anyway, then resolutely stepped onto the first step leading up to the courthouse.

And his brother's fate.

Forty years.

Tim trudged down the street from the courthouse, his hands in his jeans pockets, like a dead man.

He could see, but despite the sunlight shining down and the brisk cleanness of the springtime air, the world was just a blur of shadows.

He could hear, but the whizzing of cars and the rumble of conversations from other pedestrians around him was muted, as if he was wearing earmuffs.

The world had lost form, muted and shadowed by the enormity of the concept that he was still struggling to come to terms with, even now almost an hour after the judge handed down the sentence.

Forty years.

Next time he saw his brother in the real world, Sam would be almost seventy.

At twenty-two, that was something Tim just couldn't wrap his head around, and it left him with a leaden weight of despair in his gut as he walked, aimlessly toward...somewhere.

He hadn't bothered with an Uber when he left the courthouse. Wasn't sure he could have thought how to even request one.

He just turned right...and walked.

And tried not to think, though the thoughts kept coming regardless.

Forty years.

What was he going to do?

When their parents were killed in a car crash when Tim was thirteen, Sam left college, came home, and got a job to provide for Tim while he finished up Junior High and High School. Since then, he had been the rock Tim leaned upon every time he needed help, or a comforting hand, or just a kick in the ass.

Now he wouldn't be there...

Also, what was *Sam* going to do?

Sam wasn't a criminal. He'd never been in trouble in his life, until he left the bar he and his buddies had been hanging out in and turned left when they turned right. He made another turn and ran into a guy in ratty clothes holding a gun on another guy, who was begging for his life.

Sam always had a gun with him. State law said he wasn't supposed to in a bar, but the Constitution is the law of the land, not the whim of a tyrant in a local state house.

When he saw that guy trying to kill the man who was begging, Sam pulled his weapon and ended the threat.

The guy he saved didn't thank him; he hauled ass away.

When the cops showed up, Sam learned the guy he shot was an undercover, and he quickly found himself cuffed and booked, charged with killing a police officer, along with a ton of lesser included felonies...and the misdemeanor of carrying while under the influence.

If his case had been tried twenty miles away, across the state line, he would have been tried under the reasonable man theory based on what he knew at the time. But here the law for defense of others still put the knowledge of the person being defended upon the defender.

And the guy Sam defended knew he was a perp being taken into custody, so he had no right to resist the cop.

Sam didn't know that. Couldn't know that. But the law didn't care. It treated him the same as the perp.

The DA went further, though. He dug through ten years of social media and found one conversation where Sam had not shut down a racist, and used that to say that since the cop was black Sam had killed him from racial animus. That made it a hate crime.

Now Sam was an innocent man wrongfully convicted. A

righteous man sent to live with murders, rapists, and scum for most of the rest of his life.

How could he survive that?

How?

Tim wanted to scream to the heavens about the injustice of it all. To shake his fist at God. How could He allow such a thing to happen?

Fury—terrifying rage—wanted to burn through the ennui that coated Tim's soul as he walked. But those fires flickered impotently against the armor of numb disbelief that encompassed his conscious mind.

The anger was there. He felt it; lived it; was it.

But he could not give voice to it.

It was like something another person was feeling. Something he acknowledged from a distance, but didn't fully experience.

And so he walked.

He lost track of how far he walked, and for how long. But when he finally looked up from the sidewalk ahead of him, the sky was dim, almost fully dark. The area was lit by streetlights and the signs above the entrances of the various shops and parlors that lined the city street ahead and to each side of him.

Tim blinked. Where was he? How far had he come?

He'd walked for hours, that was clear. But in which direction?

He didn't recognize any of the stores on this block, or the street—two-laned and moderately trafficked—at all.

Tim went to turn around, to get back to a place he knew, but stopped when his eyes landed on the storefront directly to his right.

It was brightly lit, and constructed in an old-fashioned manner that evoked images of comfortable diners. Through the large windows on the storefront, he saw white tables, surrounded by pastel-colored chairs, and a glass-covered display counter in the back. Baked goods were in the case, and an elderly woman in a flowery dress with a white apron overtop held court behind the counter.

The sign over the storefront wasn't lit but somehow it was still easily readable: Miss Melody's Cafe.

Though he was still outside, the place radiated warmth, comfort, and welcoming attraction, and Tim could not help but step toward the swinging front door.

Then he was inside, and arpeggiated classical guitar music swept over his body from speakers he could not see.

The fragrance of baked bread, and other more sweet pastries that he could not name, flooded his nose, along with a comforting warmth that somehow was lacking in the streets outside.

Immediately it was like the tension in his body was leaving him, and he walked slowly toward the counter in back.

The woman there had her grey hair up in a bun atop her head. Her round face turned toward him as he approached, and she put on a smile of welcoming compassion as he came to a stop in front of her.

"Good evening, dear. I'm Miss Melody," she said.

"Hello," Tim replied, by rote, though he had no idea what to really say to her.

She seemed to understand, and nodded at him, then bent over to pick something up from behind the counter. When she straightened, she had a platter of cookies in her hands.

Chocolate chip, and apparently freshly-baked. One of them was broken in half, and the chocolate of the chips inside it was running, still hot and smooth from the oven.

Miss Melody extended the plate across the counter toward him.

Tim reached out toward the cookies by instinct, but stopped

before he could take hold of one. He looked back toward her. "How much?"

Her smile increased a fraction. "First time visitors are free dear," she said, and it seemed the air rang with her words for a heartbeat.

Tim nodded thanks, then selected one of the cookies and raised it to his mouth.

It was warm. As warm as advertised. And moist, and chewy, and the chocolate ran smoothly as he bit into it just as its companion's innards had spilled so easily onto the plate.

The sweetness swept from his tongue through the rest of his body in a spasm of bliss that swept the numbness, and the fiery anger beneath, from him as though it had never existed.

For a time he was lost in the sensation of biting, chewing, and swallowing, and that was the entire span of his universe.

Only that pleasant warmth, the ecstatic flavor.

But then after a few moments, the cookie was gone. Tim opened his eyes—he hadn't realized he had closed them—to find Miss Melody looking at him patiently with a kind smile still on her lips.

"Feeling better, dear? Would you like some more?"

Tim opened his mouth to say yes, but then his cell phone beeped in his pocket. He flinched, then pulled it out and looked down.

It was a text from Shania, his girlfriend.

The latest, of more than a dozen, over the last several hours.

"Where are you? Are you ok?"

The time at the top of his cell phone screen took him aback. He had been walking for a good five hours. And he was supposed to meet up with her an hour and a half ago.

He'd blown her off without realizing it, and now she was worried about him.

"No thanks," he said, not looking up from his phone. "I gotta go."

Somehow he registered Miss Melody nodding in response, though he wasn't looking at her. "I understand," she said. "Come back any time."

Something in her voice made him look back up at her, and he did so just in time to see her pull the top page off of a calendar pad that was set up to his right atop the counter.

It was one of those pads that showed the current date, and could be pulled off easily. And when she did so he could have sworn he saw little golden-yellow sparks fly away from the adhesive joint where the pages were bound together, for a second.

Miss Melody held the page out to him and he took it.

Glancing down, he saw the date dominated the page in bold, easy-to-read letters. At the top was Miss Melody's Cafe in the same script as on the sign out front. Below the date was the image of Jesus holding a lamb in his hands, walking with apparent confidence and tender care from knee-high grass.

"The Lord is my shepherd," was written in script below the image. Then below that was the address to Miss Melody's Cafe.

"Thanks," he said, and looked back up and her and smiled in a way he hoped was grateful. "I'll do that."

She nodded to him, and he turned to go.

When he reached the door, a bell overhead rang when he pulled it open. He couldn't remember the bell from when he came in, but he cast that from his mind and stepped across the threshold.

The world dissolved into golden-white light.

He was sitting in a small room with a set of bunkbeds on one wall. The walls were whitish-grey, and dirty as though they hadn't been cleaned in quite some time. There were no other furnishings in the room except for a seatless toilet against the rear wall, and a small sink adjacent to the toilet.

He was on the lower bunk, and another man was next to him. They both were wearing orange prison jumpsuits. The man was Hispanic, and bearded, about forty-five years old with a closely-cropped beard and brown eyes. He had a book open on his lap, and was running a finger along one page as he read.

"...he was crushed for out iniquities; the punishment that brought us peace was placed upon him, and by his wounds we are healed."

The man looked up from the page at him, his eyes narrowing slightly. "Do you understand?" he asked.

***

He was standing in a common room next to the Hispanic man. The man was about five years older now, but still strong and vibrant. There was a group of ten or fifteen men seated in chairs looking at the Hispanic man while he stood, holding the book and reading from it.

He watched from his friend and mentor's side, feeling pride in his friend's ability to speak the word, but also joy that he could participate and assist.

***

He stood next to the Hispanic man, now much older as he lay on the floor convulsing. Men in blue guards uniforms pushed him aside to get to the Hispanic man, and others in clothing that labeled them medics followed. Then checked the Hispanic man over, then put him on a stretcher and wheeled him away.

His Bible lay on the floor where he had lain, forgotten in the haste to get him out of there.

He was sitting in another cell in the prison, just like the first. Another man sat next to him. This man was younger, just barely in his twenties, and blond, with piercing green eyes and a perpetually haunted expression on his face.

He read from the Bible, the same passage his Hispanic friend had used all those years ago to help bring him to peace and faith. And over the minutes he saw the young blond man's expression easing as he began to understand the message.

The blond, green-eyed man was older now, standing at his side as he addressed a gathering of twenty or thirty men in orange jumpsuits, all gathered in the common room. The TV was going behind them but no one paid attention.

One man tried to barge in, to watch something, but all eyes turned on him and he quickly faded away.

Then they looked back at him, and he read to them.

"The Lord is my shepherd, I shall not want. He makes me lie down in green pastures..."

He walked out of the prison, in clothes he no longer recognized but somehow still fit him after all these years.

His eyes alighted on Tim, accompanied by his bride, still as beautiful as the first time he met her when they came together to talk to him at visitation time, after they decided to get married. Their children were with them, grown now. With the grandchildren, they made quite a brood awaiting him in the parking lot.

Seemed like they took up half the place.

Tim walked toward him apart from the others, and they met, and embraced, and he felt joy. Joy at release, and at being with his brother and his family again.

But not joy for freedom. He had been free for years

The world dissolved away into blackness, then a single spark of golden-light came into being; Sam's face was easy to see within it.

From that spark of light showered dozens...hundreds...more. The faces within them were unrecognizable, but at the same time somehow familiar. Faces of men that Sam had helped lead to truth, peace, and the joy of true freedom even while within physical bondage.

The faces rushed past. One after another after another, in a stream that seemed like it would never end.

Tim staggered backward as the world snapped back into place around him, the kaleidoscope of faces in golden white abruptly returning to the calm, warm, interior of Miss Melody's cafe.

For a minute or so he just stood there, stunned.

Had he seen—?

Was it real—?

He shook his head, then looked back toward the old woman behind the counter. She just looked at him, the same kindly smile on her face.

"Feeling alright, dear?"

Tim blinked, then realized that yes, he did feel better. He nodded. "Yes. What was... Was that real?"

Miss Melody didn't reply, just raised an eyebrow at him.

His thoughts whirled. Had he seen the future? Seen what Sam would experience—some of it, at least?

If that was so...no, it couldn't be.

"What is this place?

Miss Melody just pointed up and behind herself, to where the same sign as hung above the place out front hung. But now he noticed the text underneath the cafe's name. "Food for the body. Healing for the soul."

Tim shook his head, trying to make sense of it. He couldn't believe that what he had just seen was real. But at the same time...

At the same time, the anger—the fury—over his brother's fate was gone.

Well, not completely gone. It would never be gone for as long as he lived; he knew that. But it was reduced from a towering blaze, that had only not overwhelmed him because of his own disbelief, into a glowing ember. An ember that he knew instinctively that he could control, and use to fuel something good.

But above all that...was peace. Peace he didn't think he'd be able to feel again, the assurance that it was all going to turn out right, for lack of a better word, the way God intended.

Tim wasn't sure how he could believe that but still not believe that what he had seen and felt was real. Maybe it was.

But that peace was real; he knew that much.

He shook his head, then focused in on the old woman again. "Who are you?"

"I told you, dear. I'm Miss Melody."

That didn't answer the question. But the finality of her

voice said she would give no better answer. So instead of pressing it, he said, "Can I come back?"

"We are always open to souls in need," she replied.

He nodded, then he turned away, toward the door.

His cell phone chirped again as he stepped through out onto the street. He looked at it again; Shania, of course.

He'd have to go deal with her. But somehow he didn't feel the urgency he had a moment—a lifetime?—ago. For a second, he didn't know why.

Then he realized; it wasn't her face he had seen beside him through Sam's eyes.

Tim spun around and looked back at Miss Melody's Cafe. And it wasn't there.

The store behind him was a smoke and vape shop.

"What the—"

He looked down at the piece of calendar paper that he still held in his left hand, and blinked when he saw that it had changed.

The date was the same, and the picture of Jesus carrying the lamb. But the address had shifted. Now it just read, "Wherever needy souls are located."

He looked back up at the totally normal storefront in front of himself, and swallowed. Then he opened up the Uber app on his cell phone.

He wasn't sure what his next step was going to be. But he knew one thing: whatever happened, he was going to be alright. And so was Sam.

He wanted to meet Sam when he came out from prison; meet him the way that vision showed he would.

So he put the numbness and the anger aside, and turned to face forward.

WATCHING BIG BEN

This spring I took a writing workshop about how to write time travel romance stories. This first story I was assigned to write for the workshop had the limitation that the traveler could not go more than ten years into the past.

So naturally, my character had to go back to watch the Steelers win the Super Bowl. Because of course she would.

Enjoy!

The car stopped and Megan looked out the front passenger seat window at a low, modern-looking two-story building set back from the road by a parking lot sized for two rows of vehicles, mostly empty at this early hour.

It didn't look like much. Grey stone that was faintly illuminated by the sun just peeking over the mountains to the east of San Diego's Sorento Valley. Dark vertically-cut windows that made the building look almost like a weird dental picture, the way the windows evenly split the otherwise unbroken grey.

Blue and silver lettering that was still illuminated by the nighttime lights behind the letters at the building's roofline read "Replay Systems, Inc."

Nothing out of the ordinary in this place; it could have been any of a hundred similar tech or biotech labs in the area. But looking at it sent a shiver of mixed excitement and apprehension up her spine.

A black and yellow duffle bag, emblazoned with the Pittsburgh Steelers Logo on the side, laid on her lap, and she flexed her fingers around the bag's handles, feeling the tension in her arms build and release slowly with each flexion.

"You're crazy, you know that?"

Kelly had driven her from her apartment in North Park, and hadn't said a word the entire drive until now.

Tearing her eyes away from the fateful building, Megan gave her a smile that she hoped was cheerful despite the nerves that were building up within her. "You've said that a dozen times now."

Kelly bobbed her head, and her blonde bangs swayed above her eyes in counterpoint. "Well you are. You're going to hop into...a time machine? Just to go back to watch Ben Roethlisberger win the Super Bowl in 2006?"

Megan didn't reply; just looked at her. They'd had this

conversation before, but she knew Kelly wouldn't be happy unless she got to say her piece...again.

"A game you watched on TV as a kid, and that you've re-watched at least twenty times since then."

"When I was ten."

"Whatever, you've seen the game. You know how it turns out."

"But I didn't get to *go*. Now I can."

"But you could go anywhere. Any*when*! And you're wasting it on this?"

Megan shook her head. "The equipment is limited. It can't take you back more than twenty years." She shrugged. "Nothing else I want to see in that timeframe."

Kelly just stared at her for a second. Then she snorted and threw up her hands. "I can't believe I'm letting you do this."

Megan smiled again, with less effort than before as her friend's concern spread warmth through her that cancelled out at least part of her nerves. She reached over and placed her hand on Kelly's shoulder and gave it a gentle squeeze.

"Don't worry. It's been well-tested. I'll be fine."

Kelly's yellow-brown eyes softened, and Megan saw the beginnings of extra moisture begin to well up for a second. Then she sniffed and placed her left hand atop Megan's and returned the squeeze.

"Just promise me you'll be careful."

Megan smiled more broadly now. "I will."

Then she opened the car door and stepped out into the brisk chill of the early spring morning. Low-50s, practically arctic cold to native San Diegans, but t-shirt weather in her home town of Pittsburgh.

She stood for a minute, breathing in the clear scent of the undisturbed morning air, hearing the call of some bird or other behind her and to the left.

Then she looked back at her friend behind the steering wheel and gave a thumbs up. "I'll be back in about 30 minutes."

She didn't wait to see Kelly's rolling eyes. Just closed the car door, hefted the duffle bag, and stepped forward toward the building, and her adventure into history.

Ford Field in Detroit looked a lot different than the TV made it appear. Older, more run down. But maybe that was just her 2023 eyes.

Even though she'd been alive in 2006, she hadn't fully anticipated the utter differences between what she was used to.

No cell phones. Or at least, the ones people had were antiques. Clunky cameras, probably many were still film.

That alone was almost like an alien landscape as she looked around the stadium during the game. Intellectually, she knew the iPhone hadn't even been invented in this time period. But still, seeing it...

Or rather, not seeing most people hunched over their phones texting or reading or watching a video made her instinctively wonder what was wrong. Several times during the game, she found herself reaching for her phone, wanting to record something for her Instagram.

Only to find it wasn't there; she had of course left everything from her time back in the Replay Systems building. She'd only brought her Steelers garb and her Terrible Towel, which she'd brought in the duffle bag.

And a winter coat.

It felt like missing a part of herself, not having the phone with her. Unnatural.

But also somehow freeing.

She found herself drawn into the game, and into the

emotions and dynamic of the crowd, in a way that she couldn't remember experiencing from the games she'd gone to back in the future.

Because she'd put the phone and the screen between herself and actually experiencing?

That thought came to her in the middle of the 3rd quarter, and it left her slightly off-kilter for the rest of the game. It wasn't a thing she had expected to consider at all.

As the game drew to a close, she found herself more pensive than exuberant despite the exultations of the Pittsburgh faithful all around her. She had made sure that her package with Replay Systems had included a ticket with them. And certainly that had made the game more fun. But now...

The happy throng of the faithful filed out of the stadium and she went with them, absorbing their energy—and enjoying it. But not as much as she thought she would before she made the trip.

She kept patting at her back pocket; kept feeling the insignificant weight of her phone not being there.

And somehow kept feeling disjointed because of it.

Her mind whirled as she walked along with the crowd, a kaleidoscope of thoughts and feelings sweeping past her.

The happiness that she had expected, to finally be here in the flesh and see this event that had mattered so much when she was a kid...that was there. It buoyed her, and she could see her father's smiling face as he watched his favorite team win, they way he had looked back when this event had first happened. Before...

She forced her thoughts away from that road, and the loss and heartache that it would inevitably lead to.

So she just walked, and followed the crowd, listening to the boisterous comments of the other Steelers fans around her and enjoying the moment.

At some point she found herself in a sports bar a few blocks from the stadium. It was a mixed crowd. Lots of Steelers fans, all smiles. A bunch of Seahawks fans, less obviously happy since their team had lost but still seemingly enjoying being there. And the rest just general football fans who had come along for the Super Bowl ride because football.

Megan managed to squirm between two groups of Steelers fans who were each engaged in their own boisterous conversations, and found a gap at the bar between a guy in a Seahawks jersey and a woman in, of all things, a business suit.

The bartenders were swamped, but Megan had found over the years that her curly black hair and sharp green-blue eyes helped her stand out in the crowd. And sure enough, in moments, one of the male bartenders—of course—took her order and spun to face the taps behind the bar to fill it.

Yeungling, of course. Gotta celebrate a Pennsylvania victory with a Pennsylvania beer.

The guy brought it back, and she paid with some of the currency Replay Systems had given her.

It wasn't counterfeit; they had apparently scoured banks and who knows where else to get real bills that would work in this time. Wouldn't do to slip a 2020 dollar to a business in 2006, right?

But then, Megan considered she didn't know for sure that it wasn't counterfeit. How would she be able to tell, and what consequence would there be to anyone—even the business—if it was? Not like the Feds could prosecute them based on payments made seventeen years before her trip if they ever found out about it.

Another train of thought she hadn't considered until she made the trip, and Megan found she was frowning as she took a sip of her beer.

"You don't look so happy for a girl whose team just won."

She gave a little jerk and looked to her left, and found the guy in the Seahawks jersey was looking at her with a raised eyebrow.

He was tall, but not dark. Brown hair instead of black; but he was handsome, she had to give him that. And he filled out that jersey nicely.

She swallowed and shook her head quickly. "Just had a weird thought is all."

He cocked his head to the side slightly. "Care to share?"

Megan took a closer look at him. His smile was broad, friendly, and his eyes sparkled, reflecting the illumination from the big TVs behind the bar and above the taps so that he looked genuinely interested.

Interested in getting into her pants anyway.

She glanced down at the watch Replay Systems had given her to wear. It showed local time, of course. But at the bottom it also showed how long she had until the recall signal would transmit and she'd be yanked back home to the bright and glorious future she had left a few hours ago—just now in that time.

10 minutes left, and she found herself frowning again. Such a short time...

"I was just thinking how much my Dad would have loved this. Being here." She shocked herself by saying that. She hadn't intended to, though it was true. Dad would have loved this.

But she hadn't even been thinking that.... Had she?

"He couldn't make the trip?" the guy asked, and took a sip from his bottle of Bud Light.

She shook her head again. "No, he's dead. Died when I was twelve."

He blinked and lowered his bottle down onto the bar, his smile slipping. "I'm sorry. I didn't mean—"

Megan waved off his statement. "It's all good. He's been gone a long time and—"

It struck her then that her dad wasn't dead. Not now, in this time. Not here.

She had come back to see the football game, the game he'd loved, to the night that had given him the most happiness she'd see in him in all the time from this night to the day he died of cancer a year and a half from now.

She'd come back, and hadn't even thought to come see him. To talk to him, even for a moment.

Right now he was in Pittsburgh, tucking her girlhood self into bed. And then he and Mom were going to maybe have another beer. Or maybe make love.

And here she was, in the place he never got to go, so completely self-absorbed that she hadn't even considered maybe seeing him and not the game.

But see him how, the voice in her head said, the logical part that had seen Back to the Future and knew the danger inherent in making contact with family while back in time.

All the same, she hadn't even bothered. Hadn't even considered it.

Her vision was becoming blurred, from tears she realized, and she flushed with embarrassment.

Megan looked away from the man and took a long, deep draw from her glass. She willed him to look away, go elsewhere, since the tears were still welling; she could feel that her cheeks were wet now.

"Doesn't look like it's all good to me," he said.

Megan took a long breath and shook her head. "It's just..." She looked down into her beer, struggling to put her thoughts and feelings together again.

She saw her father's face, so joyful that night.

"He loved the Steelers. Seeing them win...it was the greatest thing for him. He used to tell me about the glory days back in the 70s, but I didn't understand it. I was just a little girl. But when we watched Big Ben win together, I saw his face, and…" She sniffed, then took another drink. "I just wanted to feel that way again."

Silence from the guy to her left, but she was in her own zone now. "We'd talked about going to the big game some day. But he died, right before Ben won it again. And…" Her voice broke and she felt the tears flowing freely now.

More silence from beside her.

It took her a moment to get herself back together. Wipe her eyes. When she finally looked back up at the guy she put on as much of a smile as she could. "I guess that sounds—"

The look on his face stopped her words in their tracks.

His eyes were narrow, his lips compressed into a deadly serious expression. "When did he die?"

"October 2007. Why—?" And she stopped, her mind going completely blank with shocked understanding as adrenaline flooded through her system.

Oh shit, she said silently. What had she done?

The man nodded slowly. He set his Bud Light down onto the bar with his left hand, and with his right reached into the thigh pocket of the cargo pants he was wearing.

He withdrew a black rectangular object and held it up in front of her. "Do you know what this is?"

Megan blinked, and felt her mouth drop open. "An iPhone. What the—?"

He shook his head. "No, it's a Samsung Galaxy S10." His eyes narrowed into squints. "Where are you from? When?"

Megan swallowed, unsure how to proceed. Clearly this man was not from here and now either; but how? Why?

Silly question, the voice in her head said again. You're here. Others will be too.

Mechanically, as though her jaw and vocal chords were acting of their own accord, she heard herself say, "San Diego. March 2023."

The man nodded, then he grinned broadly. "So it really does work." He sounded triumphant, but also relieved, like a weight of worry had fallen from his shoulders.

"What do you mean? You're here. From...?"

"San Jose. January 2019. I'm the CEO of a startup. I wanted to be the first to try our equipment; it's my baby so I should take the risk."

"Replay Systems?"

His eyebrows rose high onto his head, and he nodded. "Thomas Schulz," he said, and held out his hand to her.

Megan couldn't believe this was happening. Numbly, she took his hand and found he had a firm, but not overpowering, grip. "Megan—" The alarm beeping from her watch cut her off, and she looked down to see the return timer counting backward from thirty seconds.

Thomas seemed to understand what was happening immediately, and he took her by the arm. Pulling her firmly, he led her to the rear of the bar, where a side corridor turned right into the bathrooms.

"I want to talk to you again, Megan. Look for me when you get back."

They reached the side corridor just as the alarm sounded again. He hustled her around the corner, and then the world exploded into a kaleidoscope of color.

When the swirls of colors subsided, Megan blinked and took a step forward.

She was back in the transport room, as the Replay Systems

staff called it. The room was about twenty feet on a side, and painted white on the walls and ceiling. It was sparsely furnished for its size; just a black table with four chairs near the wall across from her and a pair of computer desks off to the right.

Behind her stood equipment racks that supported the transport, and she stood on a black pad that was raised off the floor by about three inches.

That was it.

As she stepped off the pad, the staff member who had escorted her in stepped forward to meet her.

The staffer was an older Korean woman—Susie—in a navy blue suit skirt and white blouse that was unbuttoned at the collar. She had her hair tied back in a ponytail and wore square black-rimmed glasses. She had been standing next to the table, clipboard clasped in both hands.

The same place she had been standing when the technicians at the computer desks had initiated the transport process, six hours ago from Megan's point of view.

Maybe a second or two ago from Susie's.

Susie reached Megan's side and smiled with professional kindness. "How do you feel?"

Megan shook her head. "Fine, I guess." She sniffed, and realized her nose was still a bit runny from her earlier crying. "It worked."

Susie nodded. "Now there may be some disorientation over the next few hours. That is normal. But if it lasts more than—"

The door off to the left, the room's only entrance, opened, and a man stepped in.

He was in a charcoal grey business suit and had lines on his face that he hadn't had in the sports bar, and there was a hint of grey in the hair on his temples. But Megan immediately recognized Thomas Schulz.

His eyes locked onto her as he strode toward her and Susie.

For her part, Susie's eyes bugged out. "Mr. Schulz!" she said, in obvious surprise.

"Thank you, Susie," he said, not taking his eyes off of Megan's as he came to a halt in front of her. "I'll take Miss Caldwell from here."

Megan felt herself flushing under the intensity of his stare.

Susie nodded and stepped back, then set her clipboard on the table and turned to exit the room.

"Hello Megan," Thomas said, and the same twinkle in his eyes from the sports bar returned. "It's good to see you again."

"You too. I guess. But—"

"But to you we only just parted company. Well, for me it's been four years." He smiled then. "I've been looking forward to this for that whole time."

She had no response to that.

He swept his arm out, toward the door. "Shall we get a cup of coffee and talk?"

Megan found herself nodding. Why not?

He nodded as well, in satisfaction. He opened the door and held it open for her, and she stepped through.

EYES OF GOLD

The second story assignment for the time travel romance work-shop was more open-ended. Thus it took me a little while to decide exactly where my traveler would go. The Roman Empire beckoned, of course, but where exactly and when?

Then it hit me. How about we go back to witness Saint Paul's appearance before the Areopagus in ancient Athens?

Sounded like a good plan, so off my traveler went.

Enjoy!

J eff knew what to expect. He'd studied for years getting ready for his journey. He studied the culture until he could recite the various customs and traditions as readily as his own. Learned classical Greek to the point he could have a comfortable conversation in it, and hadn't that taken some doing.

He became accustomed with writing with a quill, and how to ride a horse.

He even learned how to swing a gladius without stabbing himself in the foot.

But when he stepped through the time portal and emerged in a copse of trees on a hilltop a mile away from Athens, he found himself rooted to the spot, his mind totally blank as he forgot everything he had learned and planned.

The heat of the early summer sun poured down upon him through a break in the canopy, and though the Greek-style garment he wore was loose and off-white, he immediately began to sweat despite the gentle breeze wafting across the land from the east.

The breeze smelled clean, more clean than anything he had encountered around Oxford, where he had done most of his studying and preparation. But there was also a hint of woodsmoke there, as well as a spiciness that he couldn't quite place.

The sky was a brilliant blue, painted only occasionally by a puffy cloud floating gently by, and the sun was almost at high noon.

He took a moment to look about; no one around, thank God. There shouldn't have been. There was no archaeological evidence of habitation in this particular spot, but really what did that mean?

He had contingency plans if someone happened to be here when he arrived: a small air gun with tranquilizer darts, which he had strapped to his chest beneath a fold in his tunic, that should put a person out for long enough to accomplish his goal. But he really didn't want to have to use it and he was just as happy that he hadn't had to.

From the pouch tied to his sash, he pulled out a small, collapsible compass and checked it. He knew the terrain from his studies. But who knew what really would be different two thousands years ago?

Satisfied that he knew north, he pushed his way through a thick bramble of undergrowth and descended the hill toward the road leading to the eastern gate of the city.

His sandaled feet felt every rock beneath their thin leather soles on his way down, and he found himself wincing after just a few hundred feet. He should have walked in them more.

But that discomfort eased when he stepped onto the Roman road. Smooth and solid now, not the pitted and worn—though still impressive—construction that he had seen and felt in his time, it immediately made for a more comfortable walk.

A moment later, he rounded a bend and found himself halting from awe again as the city proper came into view.

He had been to modern Athens. The ruins of the past were there, up on the hills above the city and elsewhere. But it was a modern city. Nothing like the expanse of classical architecture in front of him now.

Columns and arches lined the streets, all whitewashed to brilliant beauty. The Parthenon was intact, easily visible, as was the Acropolis. And hundreds of other lesser buildings that combined into a flowing thing of beauty that, to his eye, put every city of his time to shame.

And Rome was more grand still!

He had to get there someday too. But for now, he needed to focus.

He looked up at the sun again, estimating the hour. If his

calculations were correct, Paul would be making his appearance in the Areopagus in about two hours. He knew roughly where it was, but he had been careful to give himself time to reach it and get situated to observe.

He'd read the recording of Paul's discourse in the Acts of the Apostles, of course. But that could not have been a word-for-word record. He wanted to hear it all, record it all.

He needed to hurry, or he'd miss it.

Ahead, the gates of the city stood open, and a red-cloaked troop of legionnaires were marching out toward him on the road. The man leading the troop had the plumed helmet of a centurion, and the standard-bearer at his side carried a tall staff from which hung a red banner with the SPQR of Rome embroidered in golden thread.

Jeff shuffled to the right to let the column of soldiers pass well to his left and had to work hard to not shrivel from the stern-eyed stare of the centurion as the battle-hardened man, tanned and muscled, with a puckered scar that cut though the blackness of his left eyebrow, took his measure as he lead his command past.

The scent of sweat accompanied the creaking of leather and thumping of their feet as they marched in perfect unison with their commander. They were just as hard as he was if more youthful, and several of them looked him over as they passed, then looked away with dismissive sniffs.

Jeff turned to watch them go and didn't find their casual dismissal at all insulting.

He had met hard men before in his own time; even the weakest of those legionnaires would give the toughest he had met a run for his money, he was sure.

He gave himself a shake, then hurried on to the gate.

His heart was beating a hundred beats per minute at least, but not from fear of the passed soldiers.

From exhilaration. This was even better than he had hoped it would be!

He found he was smiling ear to ear as he passed within the city.

Sophia pushed the sleeves of her dress up to keep them from getting wet, then picked up the clay pitcher she had brought with her from her father's house and bent over the stone-walled pool in front of her to fill it.

The pool was a good thirty feet across, filled with runoff from an aqueduct coming down from the mountains to north of the city. The water was clear, for the most part, owing to the fact that the pool drained into ducts beneath the city streets so that it could continue flowing despite pooling here briefly on its way.

Or at least, that's what her older brother, an engineer in the service of the city, told her.

She was willing to take his word for it. Her interests lay in other areas than planning and construction, and anyway it seemed to work pretty well.

The water spilled off the last of the aqueduct's run a third of the way around the pool from where she was standing, making a continuous splashing sound that carried over the hubbub of conversation from the dozens of other people milling about the square where the pool was located.

Despite the hustle and bustle all around, she almost could close her eyes and imagine she was in the country near a little waterfall, if she focused on that splashing sound enough.

Almost. Not today, though.

It only took a minute to fill her pitcher, but she left it submerged for a time, enjoying the coolness of the water as it flowed past her forearms.

In the heat of the day, she was often tempted to just jump in the pool sometimes; she felt that now in a flash of impulsiveness.

She would not, of course. Not since the one time she'd done it as a child, and the thrashing that had earned her. Mother had taught her quite plainly—bathhouses and drinking pools are *not* the same thing.

It still pulled at her, though, if only for the mischief of it.

With a sigh, Sophia straightened and pulled the pitcher from the water. She set it on the rim of the pool for a moment to re-arrange herself before hefting it back to her father's house.

As she pulled her sleeves back down, she glanced around the square again, and her eyes alighted on a man who had stopped half a dozen paces from her. He was taller than average, clean-shaven, with a long lean face that was topped by a curly mass of reddish-brown hair that stood out against the sea of mostly black and brown worn by her countrymen.

His clothing was exceptionally well-made. The finest of fabric, and dyed a shade just off of white, fringed with blue thread. The pouch on his belt bulged; clearly he was a man of means.

But he had a look of bafflement on his face. He was scratching at his chin with his left hand as he looked first left, then right.

Sophia didn't normally bother strangers, especially strange men. But there was something about this fellow. The way he stood out so uniquely in the crowd. Or...she didn't know what it was.

Still, she surprised herself when she called out, "Are you lost, stranger?"

The aqueduct square was magnificent. The fluted columns bringing the final flow into the pool itself were precisely aligned to create a gentle slope so the fluid would not create an excessive splash when it spilled into the pool, but it was subtle enough that you almost wouldn't notice it if you only looked at one section.

The pool itself was intricately carved, with images of animals of all sorts scampering around the outer stonework, and engravings of fish in the stonework of the pool's bottom.

The square was paved in polished flagstone—though it could be marble; Jeff wasn't good at telling one stone from another—giving the entire space a formal, elegant appearance that turned the everyday task of obtaining water into an exercise in artistry.

Any other time, Jeff would be content to stand and study the work for hours. But he had already taken longer than he expected to find his destination, and he had to admit he was completely turned around.

So when the voice grabbed his attention, offering assistance, he turned to face it gladly.

And stopped dead.

He hadn't even recognized that the voice was female until he saw her. She was shorter than the norm he was used to, but that was to be expected. She had black hair that was woven into a single braid that draped down her left shoulder. Her dress, dyed a light blue, was as modestly conservative as one would expect in this time period.

But the modest tailoring could not conceal the fact that she had a wondrous figure, curved in all the right places and apparently well toned.

But what really drew him in were her eyes. Dark, as he would expect from a Greek, but with flecks of almost gold sprinkled in the deep brown of her irises.

The rest of her face of merely pretty; the eyes made her stunning.

Like the fountain, he could almost just stare at them for hours and not find the time lacking. But that would not do at all. So instead he cleared his throat and put on a friendly smile.

"I am embarrassed to say that I am, miss. Can you point me toward the Areopagus?"

She blinked, and her eyes flicked up and down his frame for a second. He felt himself being weighed and measured, and found it rather appealing for a moment.

"You don't look like a philosopher, and your accent is strange. Where are you from, stranger?"

Jeff felt himself flushing. "Pardon my manners. My name is Jeffrey. My family is from Brittania but I've traveled most of the Empire in my studies."

She nodded slowly, digesting that and apparently deciding it met with her approval. "Sophia," she said, then pointed behind him and to the left. "Go that way two blocks, then turn right and continue a quarter mile. Then left, and you can't miss it." She cocked her head for a second as though considering, then added, "I don't believe they are meeting today, though."

Jeff blinked, thrown for a loop. "I hope you are mistaken. I very much had hoped to hear a man speak there today."

"Who?"

She was awfully inquisitive, and knowledgeable about the goings on of the philosophers. Not that the latter should be a surprise; Athens was a city full of gods and philosophers after all. But women didn't typically get involved in that during this time. So Jeff found himself even more intrigued.

"A man named Paul."

She frowned, then visibly perked up. "Paul. The man from Tarsus, in Cilicia?"

"You know of him?"

Sophia shrugged. "Only through my younger brother. He's a Platonist, and likes telling me about their latest debates. But Jeffrey," she raised her eyebrows, "he told me the man Paul spoke there two days ago."

"You're kidding."

She shook her head.

"Damn."

The crestfallen look on Jeffrey's face made Sophia's heart go out to him. It was the look of a fellow who had put all his hopes on a thing, only to see it waft away into the ether.

She knew that feeling.

Perhaps that was why she didn't just let it lie and let the man go on about his business, dashed though it was.

Instead, she found herself saying, "My brother tells me he was proclaiming some strange new god, but that his words were intriguing." Sophia smiled as she recalled the expression on her brother's face when he related the tale. "Very intriguing. Justus hasn't been able to stop talking about it, or him, for two days."

Jeffrey nodded emphatically. "I would be shocked if he wasn't enthralled."

"You know of Paul's teachings?"

"Only through writing. I've never met the man, or seen him speak." Jeffrey's eyes went distant, and he turned to look in the direction of the Areopagus, frowning. "I am very sorry to have missed it."

"Well I am certain Justus would enjoy talking about it with you if you had a care to."

Jeffrey blinked, then looked at her, his expression guarded. "I would not seek to impose."

Sophia found herself laughing at that. Not at the man's

polite consideration, but at how unneeded it was, where her brother and a talk about philosophy was concerned. "Believe me, if Justus were to find out that you had more understanding he could delve into and I *didn't* invite you to speak with him, I would never hear the end of it."

Jeffrey nodded slowly, thinking it over. Then he made a little frown that screamed regretful refusal. "I've come all this way," he said. "I simply can't not see the Areopagus, at least."

That was odd. Not like he couldn't visit it tomorrow, or the day after, or any time when they met to debate next. Was he just going to go through weeks of travel from wherever he came from last just to turn around and leave so quickly?

Strange idea. And more strange was the pang that sent through her, for a moment.

After all, why should she care if this fellow she met moments ago stay or go?

But looking at him, the earnestness on his face, she found she didn't like the idea of not seeing him again.

"If you change your mind, he is helping me care for our father in his last days. His house is up that street three blocks," she pointed the direction. "Ask for the house of Apollios."

Jeffrey smiled at her, and it lit his face up. "Thank you, Sophia. I may just do that."

***

All the way to the Areopagus, Jeff kicked himself mentally.

Clearly his calculations had been badly wrong. Two full days off! But how? He had been meticulous, double-checked every record, every reference, every variable.

To have come all this way and miss the very target he came for? It was infuriating.

The analytical part of his mind pushed back on that train of thought. After all, being accurate to within two days over the span of two thousand years was quite good. Admirable work, all things considered.

Except that it meant his mission, his entire purpose for coming here, was a failure.

So he told the analytical part of his mind to shut up, and he stewed.

He stewed so hard that he barely noticed the intricacies of the Areopagus' design and construction; artistry matched with practicality to precisely match the purpose for which it had been created.

As he walked away from the, admittedly magnificent, structure, he felt in a daze from the disappointment still.

The chronometer that he'd synchronized with the time portal's telemetry limiter was tucked away next to his air pistol. He took a moment near the side of one of the streets to fish it out and have a look.

Four and a half hours until the limiter's window closed, and he would be unable to open a portal back to his own time.

He could open the portal at any time up until then, but only at the target location where he had arrived. Now that he knew the way better, he was sure he could get back there in an hour, maybe a bit less.

Might as well just go. Chalk this up as a loss and go.

Jeff turned to do just that, but then the image of dark brown eyes with flecks of gold flashed into his mind. And he paused mid-step.

Where did Sophia say her father's house was?

It was silly to remain for a lovely set of eyes. But it wasn't just her eyes that intrigued him, was it? She had a boldness, a zest about her, that struck at something in Jeff's psyche.

And really, if he had the time, it would be a crime not to see as much of this wondrous city and this wondrous time as he could. A crime against scholarship and science.

It was as good an excuse as any. So instead of heading back to the gate and his portal, he turned his steps back to the aqueduct square, and then to the street she had indicated.

When the bell announcing guests rang and Sophia opened her father's door to find Jeffrey standing in the entryway, she was shocked by the surge of pleasure that ran through her at seeing him.

Not that he was ugly. Far from it. But he was not the sort of dashing pile of handsomeness that she had always found most appealing in men.

All the same, there was...something...about him.

"Good afternoon, Sophia," he said, politely. "I hope I am not intruding."

"Of course not," she said and led him inside, then through an anteroom to a writing chamber where Justus was seated in front of his work table, quill in hand as he worked on his latest treatise.

She couldn't remember the topic. Something obscure, though she would never say that to him.

Justus looked up as they entered, and for a second Sophia was struck by how much his round face, framed by black curls, resembled their fading father's.

Much less lined, of course, and he had not even begun to go to grey and wouldn't for several years yet. But in the dimmer light of this interior room—Justus had not lit any candles, instead relying on the natural sunlight from outside—she almost forgot that their father was lying abed two rooms over, and not sitting here where he had so often in the past.

An upsurge of sadness, a preview of the grief of loss that she knew was soon to come, swept through her for a second. She forced it down. Looking at Jeffrey and gesturing toward him for Justus' sake helped, strangely enough.

"Justus, this is the man I told you about. Jeffrey, from Brittania."

Justus was up out of his seat before she had even finished speaking, his light green robes billowing in the breeze that his sudden movement created around himself.

His eyes were delighted, his smile broad and welcoming, as he greeted Jeffrey.

"I'm so glad you've come. Sophia tells me you're a disciple of Paul?"

Jeffrey blinked, then shook his head. "No, not of his. Though I know of his teachings, and follow his god."

If anything Justus' smile grew larger. "Excellent! Come my friend, you must tell me more about this man, and his god."

He took Jeffrey by the arm and began to lead him away. But he paused after a step and looked back at Sophia. "Sophia, will you bring some wine to the rear courtyard, please?"

She couldn't help but smile fondly at Justus and chuckle at his exuberance. She nodded. "Of course. Enjoy yourself."

For a second as he was being led almost bodily away, Jeffrey looked back at her, a harried expression on his face, and she laughed more loudly.

She almost felt guilty putting the poor man through this. Almost.

Sophia busied herself with preparation for the evening meal, and tending to father's infrequent requests. She lost track of the time, but the shadows had grown noticeably longer when the two men stepped back into view from the rear courtyard.

"Are you sure you will not stay for a meal?" Justus was asking as the two of them approached her.

Jeffrey shook his head. "I cannot, I'm afraid. I have another commitment this evening." He paused, then looked from Justus to her. "But I would very much enjoy seeing you again."

It seemed his eyes lingered on her longer than on her brother, and Sophia felt a little stirring of pleasure in her belly at that.

"And I as well," Justus said.

The two men clasped hands, and then Jeffrey turned to leave. He paused though, giving Sophia a direct look. "Thank you for your assistance today, Sophia. Until we meet again."

"Soon, I hope," she found herself saying, and he flashed a smile at her.

Then he stepped through the portal to the street, and was gone.

"Well," Justus said, stepping over next to her. "A very interesting man, don't you think?"

She nodded. "Yes."

Justus looked sidelong at her and grinned that mischievous smile he had mastered when he was six and she only four.

She just rolled her eyes in response. But inwardly, she knew his teasing was pretty close to the mark.

Jeff reached the hilltop, and the cluster of trees where the portal would open, without incident and with twenty minutes still to go on the limiter timer.

He stood there with the portal trigger in hand, willing

himself to activate it and get back to where he belonged. But he hesitated.

This had been a day beyond what he had expected. Glorious. Exuberant. Exciting. Disappointing. Surprising, in almost every way.

A large part of him didn't want to leave.

It was foolish, he knew. But he could not deny it.

The future he was going back to felt sterile, lifeless compared with the living artistry he had walked through all day. Yes, he had missed Paul's speech. That was disappointing. But it didn't change the overall truth of this visit: it had been amazing.

And he could always go back two days and—

He stopped mid-thought.

Could he just go back those two days?

If he did, there was a significant chance he would bump into Justus at the Areopagus. And maybe Sophia somewhere in the city on the way to or from.

That would certainly cause a paradox of some kind, because when they met him for the first time today, after already having met him two days earlier...

He knew there was lots of debate among physicists, even now with time portals a reality, about how reality would deal with such a thing. Some said it would be physically impossible to make such a trip; that the laws of the universe would step in to preclude it from happening, somehow. Others said it would branch of a new parallel universe following the changed path the second trip made.

Others said more outlandish things, getting all the more outlandish the more people weighed in.

Regardless, the protocols were hard and fast now - any potential paradox was to be avoided on pain of severe punishment.

So if anyone knew he was going back earlier and they knew

about his meetings now, they would stop him from doing it. Unless he lied, or just took a rogue trip.

But those carried their own problems.

But the more he thought of it, the issue of paradox wasn't why he found himself rejecting the idea of coming back to see Paul's speech on the actual day.

What did it was the image of dark brown eyes, with flecks of gold in the irises.

Even the possibility of messing up the timeline so they would not have met, or could not meet again...

He wouldn't do that. Couldn't.

But he would definitely be coming back. That was for certain. And he'd set the limiter for a longer window, so he wouldn't have to rush.

After all, he had the writings of Paul's speech, and his other speeches and letters. He knew what Paul had to say.

He didn't really know Sophia yet. But he found he really wanted to.

Finally he pressed the recall button, and the world exploded in a kaleidoscope of light that brought him back to his own time.

But soon, to come back again. And see where things went.

DREAM OF THE DRYAD

It rained a lot in San Diego this winter. Much more than usual. Which is great because we needed it. And it's always amusing to watch wimpy San Diegans freak out over wet roads.

But I kind of had rain on the brain when I sat down to write this story. So naturally, the character starts off getting rained on. And things just go fantasy-horror from there.

Enjoy!

teady raindrops made a drumbeat atop the raised cowl of
Norman's cloak as he trudged up the path toward his
home in the foothills above his lord's manor house and
the village adjacent to it where most of the yeoman farmers who
worked the fields surrounding the manor lived.

Many times he had been asked why he didn't live nearby to
the others. Sometimes out of curiosity, sometimes out of envy,
sometimes out of suspicion that he must be out of his mind.

Most times he pointed out that it made no sense for a
trapper and tanner to live close-in. For one thing, the agents he
used to tan the hides of the animals he caught were pungent.
For another thing, being in the woods meant it was easier to set
and tend his traps.

Folks generally nodded and let it drop, understanding if not
generally agreeing with his reasoning.

But really, Norman just didn't like being around people all
the time, and he loved the beauty of the wooded hills, the seclu-
sion of it. Just him, his dog, his work, and God's nature to fill his
soul with peace.

Would be nice to have a woman around sometimes, though.
He had to admit that.

But despite how he truly did love living up here, right then
as his boots sank deeply into mud that used to be a well-packed
path leading up to his home, and wind-driven rain splattered his
face and dripped down inside his cloak to soak the rest of him,
and the darkening evening's chill seemed to creep into his very
bones, he reflected that maybe those nay-sayers had the right of
it after all.

But that idea wouldn't do him any good right this moment.
And besides, he knew it was a lie even as he thought it.

So he kept his head down, looking toward the next few steps
ahead and trying to ignore the increasing dark that imposed

upon the dreary grey overhead as the sun slipped beneath the horizon to the east. And placed one foot in front of the other.

Just a few hundred more yards, then he would reach the top of the shallow rise he was climbing. Then a turn to the right and he'd get to his cabin, built from logs that his father had helped his grandfather fell, hew, and stack to create the dwelling that they had passed on to him.

Just a little while longer, then he could pull out the coals he had stashed away into a warming dish beside his stove, shove them within and feed them some kindling and tinder, blow on them to produce a flame, and then feed it with the larger fuel he had stacked in the corner as the retarded but not smothered flame renewed itself.

And then, blessed, glorious warmth.

Not long now.

The rain seemed to increase with the encroaching gloom, and the oaks and elms lining the track up to his home began to take on sinister shapes all around him. The smell of water in the air seemed to become sour, rank, like some poison had leached into the rainfall itself.

Foolishness. Norman shook himself, sending his own shower of droplets that fell in tandem with the rain as his cloak shed, for a heartbeat, the burden nature had imparted to it.

But only for a second.

Then the impact of the drops upon his head was all, and the gloom continued to deepen.

Overhead, the clouds seemed to lower, their grey wanting to swallow up what little remaining light there was, and he heard the rumbling of thunder off in the distance.

Then closer, and flashing of lightning began to illuminate the track ahead and the trees of either side in fleeting but brilliant white-blue instants that made him blink from the sudden contrast with the dark of the approaching night.

He should never have stayed at the harvest feast as long as he had. He knew how long it would take to get home, and the building clouds had foretold the rain that would make his trek into a miserable slog.

But Helena had made a batch of her special mead and offered to share it. And that desire for a woman's company which he had felt so often but never fully pursued enticed him to stay.

Her golden curls, and the way the sunlight glinted in her blue-green eyes. The graceful sway of her hips as she danced with him before the lord's retinue of musicians on the green... those had convinced him to ignore the warnings that nature had given him.

And now he was paying the price in this miserable climb, and without even a kiss to show for it.

But there was the promise of that to come, the bright side of his mind reminded him. She had asked him to call on her when next he came down.

Later is not now, he replied to that voice, and growled inwardly to shut it up.

It mostly did.

All the same, the memories of his hand on her hips as they danced, and her hands on his shoulders and the gay smile on her face as he spun her, remained. And somehow that created an inner warmth that fought against the chill that threatened from outside.

But only a little.

Another flash of lightning, followed quickly by a sharp crackle of thunder, brought his eyes up from the nearly-invisible track in front of his feet, and in the brief illumination he saw the bend to the right directly ahead.

Just a few tens of yards now, and he'd be home.

So close.

He redoubled his efforts, lengthening his stride and drawing quick breaths as he felt his heart beat faster in time with the exertion.

Or was it from the memory of Helena?

He shook himself again to force the daydream—the duskdream—away, and just then another flash of lightning came. Brighter than the others, so bright he was left dazzled for a second.

The thunder came almost instantly after, so loud he stumbled backward and to the right.

He lost his footing, and pinwheeled his arms, but failed to right himself, and found himself sprawled on his right side, his fall cushioned by the soft, slimy embrace of the mud.

He laid there for a moment that stretched into a small eternity, stunned by the brilliance of the flash and the impact of the sound, and tasted mud. Felt the streaming water running down the hill flow past his body and through his hair and down his shirt, filling his boots.

And with it, the chill of night that would be nearly full if he could see anything besides the purple-yellow afterglow of the lightning strike.

His mind shrieked at him to move, to get up and get to his cabin, so close now. But he could not move. He just lay there, blinking away the afterglow and wondering when it faded but somehow still remained, in a yellow-orange flickering that ebbed and flowed over him.

It took a minute, then he realized he wasn't imagining that flickering; it was real, and not merely the remnants of the lightning bolt in his eyes. Coming from off to the left, nearby.

Norman boosted himself up onto his hands and knees and turned his head, and felt his mouth drop open.

At the bend of the track to his cabin had stood, for as long as he could remember, a stout oak, older than his grandfather, with limbs stretching higher into the heavens than any other tree for miles that he had ever seen.

He had played in that oak as a boy, climbing and exploring its limbs and knots, its twisting and growing.

Now the oak was stricken, its trunk split in two and its branches fallen and shattered. The glow was from flickers of flame that fought against the onslaught of rainfall to eat at the hewn trunk, reaching upward greedily to consume what it could before it was extinguished.

He could smell the smoke easily above the scent of rain, see clearly the wreckage of the once-mighty tree, and he realized the lightning must have struck it.

What else could have made such a wound, created such a lively flame in this onslaught of water from the heavens?

Norman forced himself to his feet, awestruck as much as he was thankful that he hadn't been closer to the tree than he had been when the lightning struck it. If he had been...

He blinked, his train of thought stopping when he saw something else in the light of the quickly-quenching flame.

There was a figure sprawled on the ground between himself and the once-mighty tree.

Slender, gracefully curved. Naked, with silver hair that covered its head and most of its back.

He knew immediately it was a woman. But what sort of woman had hair like that who was less than sixty? For surely she could not be that old. The dying fire showed plainly the youthful tint of her skin, and though she was face-down on the ground he knew immediately she would have youthful beauty such as he had never seen before.

He took a halting step forward, entranced by her, and then he stopped. Where had she come from? Surely she hadn't been up here; no one was crazy enough to be out on an evening like this.

No one but him, and he only because he needed to get back to his home.

And even he wasn't out without clothing!

Norman licked his lips and hurried to her side—more like stumbled. He squatted down to touch the side of her neck. He felt her blood pulsing through her veins, saw the rise and fall of her chest.

She was alive, but even more stunned than he had been.

He needed to get her inside, get the fire going in his stove, and get them both warmed. Then he could figure out who she was and where she had come from.

He hesitated only a moment in removing his cloak, and cringed at the renewed onslaught of rain against his exposed chest and shoulders, his shirtsleeves no proof against nature's assault.

But he was soaked already, and anyway home was close at hand. So he stooped again to wrap her in the cloak and slipped his hands beneath her shoulders and knees. Then he tensed to lift.

He stopped dead as her head turned, and in the fast-fading light of the nearly dead fire her hair parted, revealing an ear that came to a sharp point, instead of a person's normal rounding.

What was this creature he had found here?

Another flash of lightning, and another crack of thunder, and he swallowed the surge of confusion and fear that the unnatural feature sent through him.

Get inside. Figure it out after, in the warmth.

He exhaled, and pushed upward with his legs, lifting her in his arms.

Her head lolled back over his right elbow as he straightened, revealing an unconscious face of haunting beauty that put all the women he had ever seen—even Helena—to shame. And he almost forgot what he was doing for a moment.

Then the last flickering of the flame that had been trying to eat what remained of the oak went out, and her features faded into dim grayness. Greyness that would soon become black so deep he would never find his house, even close as it was now.

So he forced himself to turn away from the shattered tree, and slogged toward the dark outline of black against near black that was his home.

Another bolt of lightning flashed just as he reached his front door.

Firelight emanated from the open door of Norman's stove, sending heat and light throughout the confines of his small but comfortable home and warding off the chill and damp of the night outside.

The rainfall has slackened, going from a continuous pounding against the roof overhead into slightly arrhythmic tapping that was almost soothing. At least compared with the earlier onslaught. He sat on one of the two carved oak chairs placed around his room's single table, set between the stove and his door, and cradled a steaming mug of tea in his hands.

His wetted clothing hung from hooks on the wall near the stove so as to use its heat to assist in their drying, and he had donned a fresh tunic and leggings from the two-drawer chest-of-drawers sitting against the wall over by his bed.

Norman distinctly did not look over in that direction; the creature lying beneath the bear fur blanket topping his bed would entrance him if he did so for too long. Instead, he just looked at the flames within the black iron of his stove and inhaled the vapors coming from his mug, occasionally sipping the slightly-spicy fluid it contained.

Sipped, and thought.

The woman, whoever and whatever she was, had been remarkably light in his arms, her figure arousingly wondrous and soft, and try though he might, he could not get his mind off the memory of how she felt when he had carried her.

How she had looked when he slipped her beneath his blankets to get her warm.

Not that he had ogled. But seeing was impossible, just as it was impossible to unsee.

She was definitely a woman, with the curves and hips and breasts to prove it. But she was not human. The pointed ears proved it, as did the slightly sharpened teeth that had been revealed when her lips parted slightly as he laid her down in his bed.

Not deadly-sharp like the teeth of a predator, but more angled and pointed than any man or woman's teeth could be.

Part of him had wanted to throw her back outside into the rain when he saw those teeth. But the tranquil expression on her sleeping face, and the haunting beauty of that face, stayed his hand.

Unnatural as she was, he could not believe she was evil, or unclean in some way.

But what was she?

A rustling from over to the side drew his eyes away from the flames in his stove, and he saw one of her arms stretch up from under his blanket. A soft moan, not from discomfort but the sort of moan a person makes when she is stretching out of a good sleep, issued from the strange woman.

Norman fought back the impulse to rise and move to her side; whoever she was, whatever she was, finding a stranger's face looking down on her as the first thing she saw when she woke would not be a pleasant thing.

Besides, maybe he was wrong about her nature. If so, having some distance from her would not be imprudent.

The moan faded into a sigh that spoke of contented relaxation that—

A gasp and a little squeak, and then the woman sat bolt upright.

Norman's blanket fell off of her and the grey-pink of her nipples seemed to glow in the firelight, drawing his eyes.

But the swift movement of her head back and forth, the darting of her eyes and the expression of confusion, bordering on fright, forced his eyes away from that enticing sight even if propriety hadn't screamed at him to do the same.

The woman's eyes alighted upon him and they grew large. He could see green and blue, with yellow flecks scattered about in her irises even as she backed away as far as she could, pressing her back up against the cabin's wall, where his bed stood against it.

"Be calm," Norman said, holding out an open hand toward her and putting on a smile that he hoped was comforting even as he worked hard to not look down from her face to her bare torso. "I mean you no harm."

She gave a shake of her head and the silver-grey locks flowing past her face seemed to sway. She opened her mouth to speak, but what emerged was not any tongue that Norman knew, or had ever heard of.

Her voice was deep, almost as deep as his, and seemed to carry a harmony of three or four notes at once as she made words, but words that were a song more than a spoken language.

He felt his mouth drop open, from astonishment but also from the beauty of it.

It was language; he knew that. She was speaking; there was meaning there. And he felt like he could just grasp the edge of it. But then it slipped away, and then there was only music, and the emotion the music carried: confusion and caution but also wonder and patience that could outwait mountains even as it rested in a joy that could not be contained even if it also felt fear.

Norman found himself entranced and had to give himself a shake to pull himself out of it; though perhaps it was merely that she had stopped saying whatever it was she had wanted to say.

He placed his mug down atop the table and spread his hands. "I'm sorry, I don't understand."

She cocked her head to the side and narrowed her eyes slightly, but didn't speak again. She just looked at him with a stare that was unnerving, as much for its unwavering directness as from her apparent lack of care over her state of undress.

He smiled and rose slowly, gesturing toward his stove, atop which sat his other mug, which he had placed there earlier to keep warm in case she woke.

Moving with careful slowness, he stepped over to the stove and picked up the mug, then approached her.

She kept on watching him with that same unnerving stare, and it was only when he reached the side of his bed that he registered the true reason it was so disquieting.

She had not blinked even once.

Swallowing, Norman held out the mug to her and tried to not look like he was as unnerved as he was beginning to feel, whatever the allure of her physicality might be.

The strange woman raised her hand slowly and touched the mug, lingering for a long moment as though tasting its warmth. Then she accepted it, cupping the mug in both hand as he had been doing the moment before she woke.

Norman backed away, returning to his chair and then lifting up his own mug and taking a drink, to show it was not dangerous.

She watched, still unblinking, and then after a few seconds slowly raised her own mug and took a sip.

Her eyes widened slightly as the tea crossed her lips, then

she drank deeply. When she finally lowered the mug. her lips were turned upward into a slight smile. She spoke again, and again it was a harmony of multiple notes that could not have been uttered at once by a single mouth. And yet it was.

And again he did not understand the words, though the emotion came through clearly enough.

Unexpected pleasure, and thankfulness for that.

She stopped speaking, and Norman shrugged in response and flashed another smile at her.

A pop from the stove drew his eyes away, and he saw half a dozen embers rising on the air before the open door of the stove, where the fuel within had spat them out.

He chuckled slightly; any other night that pop might have been alarming. But after the lightning strike earlier...

The chuckle became deeper, and he turned back to the woman, only to find she had lain back down again. She was resting on her right side, the blanket still carelessly lying so it covered her hips and legs but not her torso, and her arms were curled up around herself to make a natural pillow for her head; and never mind that he had a pillow on his bed already.

Her eyes were closed again, and her chest rose and fell slowly. A soft almost-purring came from her.

Was she back asleep already, and so easily after having been obviously startled and out of sorts just moments ago?

But after another several minutes of watching her, and her not moving at all except to breath, Norman decided that it was true, strange as it might seem.

He also realized that he was drowsy as well.

Not that he had any place to lay his head, drowsy or no. His was the only bed and though it was large enough to take two he wasn't going to presume to join her beneath the blankets there.

So he sat up, thinking and sipping at his tea and watching the flames in the stove, and her, in equal measure.

The growing warmth in the cabin from the stove's heat combined with her near-purr to make his eyelids heavy though, and at some point he felt himself drifting off, his head coming to rest on his forearm atop the table in front of his chair.

Norman dreamed, but it was unlike any dream he had ever had. All feelings and tastes and scents but no images, rumblings but no distinctive sound.

He had the notion of countless years passing and yet a feeling that time did not exist at all. Just a stretching and growth, and reaching and climbing and digging deeper, a tasting that shifted from sweet to slightly sour to full-on tart back to sweet, and a warming that made his limbs stretch farther than they ever had along with a chill that felt almost as though his fingers and toes were painlessly falling off even while they still remained and he still felt them as normal as they had ever been.

Alongside all that, throughout it all, there was a sense of presence, of otherness that was also oneness, another being beside and within him, that cared for and comforted him, protected but also fed off him. Played and caressed him but also morphed him into something pleasing to that other presence.

All these feelings morphing into one, in a slumber that felt like it stretched for eons, but when he opened his eyes the fire within his stove was still burning, though only tiny flickers of flame amidst the red glow of still-warm coals.

Norman pushed himself upright and moved to stand in the dim light, but stopped when he looked to the right, toward his bed and the strange woman who had come into his life so unexpectedly, and so weirdly.

The bear fur blanket was cast aside.

She was gone.

Norman did a full turn, scanning the entirety of his small one-room home and found he was completely alone.

Only the disturbing of his blanket revealed that the woman had ever been there.

But had she been? Maybe he had imagined it. He had dreamed deeply; maybe she had been part of his dream all along. If—

A sound interjected itself into his consciousness, and Norman realized it had been there the entire time, just so subtle that he had missed it in his surprise at finding the woman gone.

A lilting harmony of notes that flowed together, carrying a tone of sorrow and loss that wrenched at Norman's heart in a way that he could not recall before.

It was coming from outside, in the woods beyond his door.

Before he even thought about doing it, he had the door open and he stepped outside.

It was chilly so that his breath misted in front of his face. After the stove-generated warmth of his cabin it was like jumping into a frozen lake, the shock of it was so great.

At least it wasn't raining anymore. But still Norman turned around to go back inside.

But the harmony was louder now, coming from off to his right. And over in that direction there was a green-yellow glow of some kind that seemed to pulse in time with the harmony's rise and fall.

It was not the sun. Through a break in the trees overhead, Norman could see stars; the rains had ended and the clouds were dispersed but dawn was still far off.

Whatever the glow was, it was off toward the bend in the path going down to the village, and the lord's manor. By the old oak.

Norman didn't notice the chill of the mud between his bare

toes as he moved in that direction, entranced as he was by the music and the radiance both.

As he drew near, both resolved themselves before him, and he realized both contained deeper resonances than he had initially perceived.

Whereas when the woman had spoken before in his house it sounded like three or four notes in harmony together, now there were six or seven. And the glow wasn't just green flashing to yellow, it was a mix of both, twining and swirling around each other and creating other lesser tones as they interacted and played with one another.

Norman stopped a dozen or so paces from where the oak stood, awe making him unable to approach any closer.

For now he could see that the woman and the tree both were the source of light and sound.

She was circling the tree, he outstretched fingers tracing along its bark and roving the wound that the lightning strike had made in the great tree's trunk. Tears of silver were running down her flawless face as she surveyed the damage, and it was like the oak was weeping as well. For was Norman seeing things or was the sap running, running freely?

Light shone from the woman's skin, yellow to match the green glow that seemed to emanate from the great tree's wound, the source of the twining glow that had drawn Norman there, her walking around the trunk the cause of the swirling.

She came to a halt with her back to him, and placed both hands against the stricken tree's trunk, fingers splayed wide as she bowed her head toward the wound, like she was going to kiss it.

"What in God's name?" Norman said under his breath, and immediately there was a discordant note to the harmony that had been emanating from woman and tree.

She stopped and turned, looking at Norman with eyes wide

and red from tears. Silver streaked her flawless cheeks, ran down her neck to her chest and streaked her breasts.

It should have marred her beauty, alienated her allure, but instead he found himself drawn to her all the more. But this time there wasn't any force pushing him, forced propriety making him look away from the lushness of her body.

Now there was invitation. To draw near, to enter in.

To merge.

Norman blinked and shook his head. What was—?

The harmony shifted as though in response to his question, and he perceived the truth of who she was, what she was.

She and the tree were one, but when the tree was struck, she was struck. Thrown from her home and into his.

The oak was dying, and if it died she would as well. But it could still be saved. Maybe. With enough love, enough strength of heart combined with faith.

She could do it...maybe—or maybe the attempt would kill the tree all the sooner, and her with it.

But if he assisted...

Norman shook his head as the invitation came again. To draw near, to enter in.

To merge.

"What will that do to me?" he found himself saying.

As if in answer, the harmony shifted again, and he found himself reverting back to his dream.

He now knew he had experienced the life of that tree; endless centuries of growth and pleasure and pain that wasn't, stretching and being. And not just the being of that one tree.

Norman's mind open to the deeper truths of that dream, and he realized he was experiencing all the being of the tree that had come before this one, and the one before that and the one before that. And the certainty that he would experience the trees to come after this one, as its acorns grew and grew.

An expanding and constantly growing experience that would not stop until the world ended or the last of the tree's descendants was torn down and burned.

Norman was moving forward before he realized he had done it; found himself standing before the lovely, alien beauty who had come so unexpectedly and weirdly into his life.

She smiled up at him, a sensuous smile that offered welcome and oneness and merging and pleasures that he couldn't imagine, offerings beyond anything a mere mortal woman like Helena could offer. And the offer would be ongoing, as long as the tree and its descendants stood.

Oneness, entrance into her core offspring from their union, and awareness eternal, or near enough to it.

As his lips touched hers, and he felt her tongue probing against his, he felt the sharpness of her teeth. And then a flash of alarm.

He tried to pull back, but arms that were suddenly rough, barklike, wrapped around him with the impeccable strength that could burrow through granite in its probing for water, deep in the soil. Strength that could withstand the strongest winds; how could he fight against that?

He could not.

He felt himself being wrapped around, enclosed in wood.

Tried to move, but could not.

Opened his mouth to scream, and roots plunged within him and down his throat.

Then there was pain, followed by blackness.

Two weeks later, a patrol of the lord's militia came up to Norman's cabin. They found the door ajar and the stove long-cold. But no sign of him.

Puzzled, they descended to the village, to report his disappearance.

They never noticed the oak at the bend in the path. How its trunk was twisted as though twined around itself. Or how the bubbling of the trunk in one spot resembled a man's face, locked into an eternal scream of terror.

Or the other section, higher up, that almost looked like a woman's face, with a look of satisfaction upon it.

KICKSTARTER HEROES

Producing this book would not be possible without the generosity of the people below, who backed it on Kickstarter. Thank you very much to all the backers. You guys are great!

Megan L

Kraggy

Mary Jo Rabe

SuperSijy

Catherine G White

Steven Crane

Datta Groover

Lyndon Perry

Jim Nealon

DDA

Tim Erickson

Undine

Anon

Cactus Eater Bear

Arkie Bear

Hans G. Shantz

Warren C. Bennet
Scire
Gridhunter
Mikkel Hogh
Jessie Beyrer
DrumMachineBear / Stephen Tyler
Michel S. Pawlowski, D.Sc., CEM
David Humphreys
David Harner

Thank you for reading my book. I hope you enjoyed reading it as much as I enjoyed writing it.

Feel free to come say hi at my website, on Twitter, or on Gab. I always enjoy hearing from readers, especially since you all are, collectively, my boss.

Also, come check out my weekly podcast, Story Time With Michael Kingswood, where I read stories and talk through some of the latest goings on in my world.

Find it on YouTube, Rumble, Bitchute, Odysee, or through your favorite podcast feed.

Subscribers are always welcome, and encouraged!

Thanks again. My best to you and yours.

Warm Regards,
Michael Kingswood

MAILING LIST

If you enjoyed this book and would like word on new releases and special deals from Michael Kingswood, sign up for his newsletter on his website. Guaranteed to be spam-free, you can opt out at any time. And you can rest assured he will not share your information with anyone, for any reason, without a court order.

https://michaelkingswood.com/newsletter-signup/

ABOUT THE AUTHOR

Michael Kingswood has published more than 80 short stories, novellas, and novels. He has appeared in anthologies from WMG Publishing, Stark Press, and Knotted Road Press. A twenty year veteran of the US Navy's submarine force, he has four children and currently resides in San Diego.

Fans can contact him through his website, on Twitter, or on Gab.

Michael has a weekly podcast, Story Time With Michael Kingswood, where he reads his work and discusses writing, philosophy, and history. Subscribers are always welcome!

Listen on: YouTube Rumble Bitchute Odysee Podcast

MORE BOOKS BY MICHAEL KINGSWOOD

Glimmer Vale Chronicles

Glimmer Vale

Out-Dweller

Tollard's Peak

Robbed Blind

The Falconer's Stairs

Campaign Season

Glimmer Vale Chronicles Books 1-3

Stories From Glimmer Vale

Legacy

Hidden Magic

Captive Hearts

Wedding Gifts

Lost Credit

The Pericles Conspiracy

Passing In The Night

The Pericles Conspiracy

Dawn Of Enlightenment

Masters Of The Sun

Novellas

What Lurks Between

The Necromancer's Lair

The Champion

Veritas Morte

Story Collections

Tales Of Adventure #1

Tales Of Adventure #2

Short Story 10-Pack

A Jar Of Mixed Treats

Short Mystery 10-Pack

Stories From Glimmer Vale, Volume 1

Stories From The Great Challenge

9 781950 683314